THE INFINITE
SUMMER

Greta Rose Evans

This book is a work of fiction. Any references to historical events, real people, or real locales are used fictitiously. Other names, characters, places, and incidents are the product of the author's imagination, and any resemblance to actual events or locales or persons, living or dead, is entirely coincidental.

So don't get any ideas.

ISBN-13: 978-1482389180

ISBN-10: 1482389185

Jeremiah 29:11

"In the midst of winter, I found there was, within me, an invincible summer."
Albert Camus

PROLOGUE

Home

We all think of a place with four walls and a roof. We all think of a place with a driveway and a house number. But what if home had nothing to do with a building?

If you asked me where home was, I would automatically respond, "211 Fairway Avenue."

But when I close my eyes, and I think of home, I don't see that sweet Victorian style house. In fact, I don't see a house at all. I see the ocean.

I close my eyes and I am eleven again. And I'm drowning.

I don't bother to keep my eyes closed; I open them and there is a world of blue surrounding me.

I'm too far down for the waves to grab a hold of me. I spent a long time getting dragged around by the sets and I've hit my head hard and I know I'm too weak to try to make it back up. I see the light dancing on the water up above but for once I don't want to follow it. I remember, in that moment, I didn't even feel as if I were losing breath or losing time; I just felt at peace. I felt like nothing could ever hurt me down there. Infinite, even. Like for just a moment the world had stopped, and I was able to grab a hold of something so much greater than myself. Like finding a sliver of gold in a charcoaled-covered world. I didn't want to let it go. I felt as if I belonged here. I was home.

That's when Clyde saved me.

ONE

If you could say one last thing to the person you loved, what would you say?

I mean *I love you* is a popular choice. But that's also sometimes extremely obvious. People know that you love them. Would you tell them that they were special to you? That they impacted you as a person? That even though they aren't around anymore, you still think about them all the time?

I used to think about this question every day. I don't know why, really. Maybe somewhere deep down I knew it was one I'd have to answer someday. Or maybe it's because I have a strange fascination with hearing people's last words. Regardless of what made it constantly pop up in my thoughts, I still was never able to come up with an answer for this question. So when I pressed my phone up to my ear, and heard my brother's frantic voice from the other end, I had no idea what to say.

"Evie, something is wrong with the plane I'm in." I could barely make out his voice over the noise in the background. It sounded as though everyone was making distressed phone calls as well.

"What do you mean something's wrong with it?" It didn't register in my mind. My brother had left that morning on a flight to Hawaii. Sure, flying was dangerous. But a plane crashing was almost unheard of, especially it being Hawaiian Airlines.

"It isn't looking too good, buddy." His voice was strained.

My brother Clyde was my best friend. Being eighteen months apart, we were practically twins. We liked the same music, wanted the same things out of life—which included adventure, to be near the ocean, and to get as far away as we could from our small town that our parents had locked us down in.
We knew as long as we had each other, we'd find a way out.

"Clyde, this isn't funny anymore. Knock it off. You're going to get in trouble if they see you on the pho—"

"No, Evie, no. This time I'm serious."

My voice was shaky. "I'm sure they'll fix the plane and it'll all be fine."

"I wish it was that easy."

It was almost frightening how calm he was. But that was my brother. Prepared to take on anything.

No matter how crazy, insane, or absolutely terrifying it was.

"Stay on the phone."

"I can't." The call was suddenly getting stat-icky. "We're falling."

"You'll be fine. You'll be fine. You'll be fine." I felt a sob working its way up my chest. The phone call didn't feel real. His voice was lingering over the line. I was so far away.

My world was spinning. I couldn't breathe.

"You will be too, sidekick. I'll see you soon."

That day I could ramble for as long as I wanted. I could tell anyone anything. I had so much time.

But some people don't. For some people, words suddenly become precious.

After that phone call, I realized it's not about what you say to them. It's about their last words to you.

JUNE

TWO

"Bling. Bling. Bling."

There are three wonderful sounds in this world that my ears indulge in. The first is the sound of the ocean, the second is the sound of the coffee maker in the morning, and the third is the sound of the bell on the last day of school.

I'm sure I was the first one out of my seat. Some people stay and linger and gossip with friends about their summer plans. But not me. There's nothing more I hate than this town and its people. I could hardly wait to get out of the school building, and yell at the top of my lungs, "I hate you all!"

As I made my way out of class, I felt someone tug at my long-sleeved shirt. I turned around slowly, already knowing who it was. "No."

Isiah's eyes grew wide. "I didn't even ask you anything."

"I don't want to go on your boat, Isiah."

Isiah is the most popular guy in the small town I live in, Mokelumne Hill. Population: 619.

Lucky me. Isiah Durante has never heard the word *no* in his life. That is, until he met me. He thinks just because he's the star quarterback and his daddy bought him a big truck he can run around the town like an obnoxious jerk and get whatever he wants.

"You don't like boats?"

"No, Isiah, I don't like you."

"Fine." His face was suddenly red with anger. "You're a bit —"

"It's Evie," I interrupted. "And thank you."

Charlotte was making her way towards me, a smirk playing on her thin lips. "Poor boy

got it rough."

I started to walk with her, leaving Isiah to pout. There was once a time when I would've put up with boys like Isiah. I might have even gone on his boat with him. But ever since my brother, Clyde, had died six months ago, I didn't have any patience anymore. Every little thing set me off.

"He doesn't deserve any sugar coating."

I met Charlotte in kindergarten. She had stolen my cubby box on the first day of school. I distinctly remember I had moved her backpack into another box, and told her to keep it there. She challenged me. Back then, she looked like a wild thing. Auburn hair sticking up in all directions. Wearing little black punk boots and a Ninja Turtles shirt. After we fought, we became the best of friends. Now she looked like a Greek goddess, with her tall frame and flawless milky skin. She always wore her long scarlet colored hair in a messy braid. Guys were drawn to her like moths to light.

She flashed a pack of cigarettes she was holding in her hand and nodded for me to follow her outside. "Kia's waiting."

As we walked down the hallway for the last time before summer started, I listened to the sound of people talking. Words like, "Australia" and "Hawaii" leaked in and out of my ears, talk of sandals and beach towels and surfing. All conversations of places far away from here. When you think of summer, you think of the sun dripping on your shoulders, the sound of the ocean, the taste of salty water in your throat. But just like every summer, I was stuck here. No way out. Nowhere to go. It left me with a sadness that was almost unbearable.

What was there to look forward to here?

As I trotted down the school steps, I pulled my hood up to avoid the rain. The sky was an ominous gray. The clouds huddled together and barely let any light through them. I sighed as I walked, and wondered whether the sun would ever come out this summer. I felt some relief when I saw Kia's red Jetta waiting out in the parking lot. Charlotte's boots squeaked as we walked towards it, and at the last minute she offered me a cigarette.

"No, thanks," I said, climbing into the passenger seat. She lit one and got into the back.

"No smoking in my car," Kia said the minute she got in.

"Oh please, Mother." Charlotte groaned, "It's just one."

"It's a nasty habit and the smell is gross," Kia said, annoyed. "Put it out, please."

Charlotte rolled her eyes and flicked it out the window.

"Well, congratulations girls, we made it another year." Kia smiled happily, like it was some huge accomplishment or something, even though it was only that we had survived sophomore year.

"Barely." Charlotte said. I knew she was being sarcastic. When you're as intimidating as Charlotte is, no one bothers you. No one says a word to you without your approval. Charlotte was strange, but it didn't matter because she was also stunning. People practically leapt out of her way as she walked down the hallways. Kia was well liked, too. For different reasons. She was kind to everyone, and lingered with so many various groups of people, it was difficult to keep track of her.

Charlotte was still fumbling with her pack of cigarettes in the back seat. "There's a party tonight."

"Of course there is. It *is* summer now."

"We *are* going, right?" Charlotte pushed.

I could see Kia's grip on the steering wheel tighten. This was our biggest problem as friends during sophomore year. To party or not to party? Charlotte practically lived for crazy nights that you couldn't remember the next morning. Kia wanted nothing to do with the party crowd. And I was still undecided.

"We'll talk about it later." Kia changed the subject quickly. "I have a proposal for you guys, anyways."

Charlotte's eyes grew wide. "Oh, great."

"Hush, Charlotte. It's good," Kia enthused.

"I'm sure it is, dear," Charlotte replied, with heavy sarcasm.

Kia suddenly chucked a book into the back seat. It was heading straight towards Charlotte's head but she dodged it. "Read it."

Charlotte looked at her, stunned. "The only book I've ever read is Harry Potter."

"The title, Charlotte. Read the title."

"Oh fine." Charlotte paused for a moment. "Mexico."

"Mexico." I eyed Kia. "What about it?"

A smile spread across her face, and she turned to me, a light glittering in her chocolate brown eyes. "I wanna go."

"And I want to date an Australian boy," I replied sarcastically. "Your point is?"

The light didn't flicker or dull; it seemed to only get brighter. "No, we're going. We aren't staying here any longer. It's time for an adventure."

Something in her voice made her sound as if she were five again. And the hopeful look in her eyes was so convincing. It was the same look that got us to be best friends at church camp when we were nine. Ever since then, it's always been Charlotte, Kia, and I. Kia has always been the dreamer.

"We're going to Soleil, right?" Charlotte asked, changing

the subject.

"Yes," Kia answered. "We can write out the whole plan there. Get the details together."

"Hey," I said, reaching towards the stereo, "we haven't heard Mumford and Son's album for a while." I pressed Play and turned up the volume, drowning out Kia's crazy idea to run away for the summer. It was impossible. There was no way.

Soleil is a cafe Charlotte, Kia, and I had been going to for as long as I can remember. My brother, Clyde, had actually discovered it in fifth grade when we were riding home on our bikes. It was just on the way to our house and it was kind of impossible to miss. Painted bright yellow, it had a big sun sign out front. They had just opened up when we went in there for the first time, and we had been going there almost every day since.

The owners were an older couple that had moved here from Los Angeles, and they had brought their beachy vibes with them. Stepping into Soleil was like stepping into a beach shack. The tables were all mismatched and there were surfboards everywhere, including one acting as the counter. Even the drinks were named after famous surf spots. Like, for instance, the vanilla chai tea I always ordered was called an RJ after The River Jetties in Newport.

Clyde had started working at Soleil freshman year. He pretty much had lived there. It was harder being in Soleil than being in my house. There was more of Clyde here. He was all about the beach, and the ocean. We used to sit for hours in the middle of the night and talk about leaving Mokelumne Hill. We knew it wasn't for us.

We'd talk about where we'd go. He always said Australia and I had always wanted to go to San Diego. As soon as Clyde had gotten his license, he randomly left for the weekend. He had told my parents he was spending the night at a friend's but I knew better. Monday morning, I begged him to tell me where he had been. All he said was, "There's this beach town, Evie. Wow, there's nothing like it."

He didn't tell me anything else after that. He promised he'd take me one day and I could discover it for myself. Thinking about Clyde hurt, and I immediately directed my attention to something else. Lorelei, the owner, was working the counter and she immediately came around and hugged us all. She held me for couple of seconds longer than the rest. There was something incredibly warm about Lorelei. Maybe it was in the way you could tell she had lived at the beach just in her complexion or that her green eyes were still glassy and youthful.

Charlotte went and sat at the table we had claimed as our own, while Kia and I ordered our usuals. It was always cold in Moke Hill, so we always gravitated towards hot drinks.

"I wish I was sipping a piña colada right about now," Charlotte joked, as I handed her her green tea.

I sat at the seat closest to the window, like always, and sipped on my vanilla chai. I would always glance between the scene around me and the scene outside. Sometimes when I was in Soleil, I forgot I was in the cold mountains. I'd pretend I'd walk outside to find sand and hear the ocean roaring. But every time I glanced at the window, I was reminded where I was. Far away from the beach.

"So..." Kia grinned, as she turned her cup of hot chocolate in her hands. "About Mexico..."

"About Mexico..." My voice faltered. "It's hot, it's beautiful. Maybe we can take a trip there when we graduate."

"Why not now?"

I pressed my fingers against the cold glass window, feeling the wetness from the rain on my fingertips and sighed. "It's not realistic."

"Are there any hot boys in Mexico?" Charlotte chimed in, playing with her braid.

"I don't know." I shrugged. "And who cares? You have a boyfriend."

"Roger is getting boring."

Charlotte had been dating Roger for two months now. There were three things that boy loved: his guitar, pot, and well, I wouldn't say he loved Charlotte. I think it was more of an obsession.

"So I was thinking airfare will probably be around one thousand for all of us, roundtrip that is...and then we really would only need a few hundred to get us through a week. We could always find a cheap hotel and—"

Even the word airplane made my stomach churn. Flying

had been one of my favorite things growing up. But I hadn't been on a plane since Clyde had died. And I wasn't sure how I'd feel about it.

"Kia," I kept my voice gentle, "I don't think—"

"And we can go surfing and walk to the little markets," she interrupted.

"Kia." This time I didn't control the annoyance in my voice. "I know you get these ideas, and you just run with them, and sometimes they work out. But not this time."

Kia's voice faltered a little but the determination didn't leave her tone. "It *can* work."

"She might be right." Charlotte pursed her lips, thinking about it.

"It can't." I was starting to get angry; how many times could I put it nicely?

"Why not?" Charlotte raised her eyebrows.

"We need money…and we need our parents to go along with it. That's not going to happen."

"I thought you guys would be on board." Kia turned her head away, a deep sense of hurt in her eyes as she realized I was serious. I didn't like disappointing her. I didn't like that I was the one who always had to speak the truth.

Charlotte piped up. "I'm totally on board."

Kia smiled happily and turned to me, a hopeful expression

back in her eyes.

"Don't make me look like the bad guy here."

"I'm not." Kia hesitated. "It's just maybe if you had a little more faith..."

"Faith in what?" I could hear my voice getting louder. "Faith in getting out of this stupid town? C'mon, we all know that's not going to happen. We're stuck here whether we like it or not!"

Kia shuddered away from my voice. "Why are you so mad?"

I could see it more clear now, the sadness in her eyes.

"I'm just tired of being disappointed." I pushed away from my chair, and left Soleil without another word.

~~

My mom's heels.

I heard them clicking down the hallway and I knew I was in for it. My mom only ever came into my room anymore when she either A—wanted to yell at me or, B—wanted to yell at me. I quickly made my way to my closet and started going through my clothes. It was always easier to take her long speeches if I was doing something. Or at least looked like I was doing something.

The click of her heels had gotten louder.

"Evelyn." I heard my bedroom door open and then close.

I started shuffling my clothes around. "Yes?"

"Oh," she said, sounding pleasantly surprised. "You're packing early."

I felt my heart stop as I turned around to face her. I tried to think of what she was talking about.

"Christian camp..." she replied to my confused expression. "Oh, Evelyn. Tell me you didn't forget."

"Okay," I said calmly, turning back around so she couldn't see my face. "I didn't forget."

I heard her sigh loudly and my bed creaked as she sat. "You go every single year."

"I know. I know." I rushed, "That's why I'm so excited to go. I must have just been so excited that I forgot!"

I had always been a good liar. I was good with my tone. Good with making things sound flowy and real. It had been one of the differences between Clyde and me. He didn't even have to speak for someone to call him out on lying. It was clear on his face. He admitted that I could've pulled off the running away incident way better than him.

My mom's composure went back to normal. "Well, I guess it isn't too early to pack. You do leave in two days. Oh, it'll be quiet without you around."

I felt another jab of pain in my chest. "It's always quiet around here now."

2>

Clyde had been the loud one. Clyde had been the one whose laughter filled the hallways. Whose guitar could be heard humming softly during the night. Whose favorite albums could be heard pouring through the open windows of his truck during the day. My parents would always tell him, "Settle down. That's too loud. Put that guitar away."

But I loved it. I loved how Clyde believed that the music should either be turned up all the way or not on at all. Now that he was gone, the silence was louder than all of that combined.

My mother and father were both lawyers. I suppose from the outside my life once looked perfect. We lived in the most beautiful house in the whole neighborhood, the one right on the top of the hill. You could see my parents' sparkly brand new cars gleaming in our driveway from the main road. Everyone knew who my parents were. And for a while the facade was kind of fun: fun to prance slowly down my stairwell in a beautiful and stupidly expensive dress, fun to impress the people at my parents' parties. It made them happy. But after a while, after we got older, we realized what bullshit it actually was. Clyde and I still went to the parties—we didn't have much of a choice—but we'd secretly poke fun at them.

When Clyde passed away, my parents still held the parties. And it almost made me feel sick. They were still so caught up in what other people thought about us. Even more so now that we had endured a tragedy.

The rest of the night involved music blasting through my headphones, coffee, and the crazy routine of checking my phone every five minutes to see whether Kia or Charlotte had tried to get a hold of me. Which they hadn't. I hadn't really expected them to. I was the one who had stormed out. I should've just gone along with Kia's plan, I thought to myself; I should've kept my mouth shut. The three of us never got into fights, and if we did, it was a five-minute bicker. There was never slamming doors or hurt feelings or raised voices. It always seemed like our personalities balanced out perfectly.

I tried to focus on other things as I turned the shower knob all the way to hot. I felt the tears start to well in my throat as I climbed in. I remember after Clyde had died. I could take up to four showers a day. My dad complained that I was going to blow up the water bill and my mom worried that I'd dry out my skin too much. But to be honest, it wasn't because I was a freak about being clean or anything like that. Have you noticed that no one can hear you crying in the shower? It's one of those simply small but wonderful things in life. In front of a crowd of people at a funeral, in a bathroom stall at school, even in the enclosure of your room, there's still a huge chance that someone will hear you falling apart.

But the water always blocks out the sound of broken, hard sobs and you can stand there for hours just letting yourself fall to pieces and no one would ever know. I let the tears stream down my face as I washed my hair, letting the comforting smell of my shampoo tranquilize me. The water brushed the tears away and I stepped out of the shower, not bothering to look in the mirror because I knew my eyes would be very red.

I tiptoed back to my room as to not wake my parents up and pulled on the pair of sweats and ratty t-shirt that I always wore to bed. I practically glared at my phone as I plugged it in to charge, unlocking it and re-locking it again and again, hoping for it to buzz with a text or a call. After a few minutes, I gave up on it. I sunk into my bed, shivered against my wet pillow from my damp hair, and tried to put my mind to rest.

"Words can't explain it." Clyde's voice echoed through my head. That's what he told me when I had asked him about his mysterious beach town. "It's simply paradise."

I drifted asleep, trying to imagine what paradise could possibly be like.

THREE

I felt sand.

I couldn't see anything around me. Everything was all blurred, just this mixture of colors. But the texture of sand was unmistakable. Gritty, yet soft. Hot on my feet.

I could suddenly hear the pull of the ocean, the sound of the waves crashing. Over and over again.

"Isn't it beautiful?"

I could hear the pure admiration in Clyde's voice.

"Yes," I said.

Because even though I couldn't see this place, I knew what it was.

I felt Clyde push something into my hand, small and sharp in some places; he closed my hand over it and I heard him move, his footsteps fading away softly.

The ocean got quieter and quieter until the sound of the waves faded into the sound of rain.

I was slowly pulled out of the dream, and as soon as I was fully awake, I felt an overwhelming amount of sadness wash over me. The weather sounded angry outside my window with the sharp sound of blustering wind and heavy rainfall. I rested my head back on my pillow, hoping I could go back to my dream, but after a few failed attempts, I forced myself out of bed. I checked my phone, but there were still no new texts or calls. I took a deep breath and tried not to be upset. It was the beginning of summer and I was trapped in the middle of a storm. I was starting to lose hope, and I really didn't know how to hold on to it anymore.

I tried my best to avoid my parents as I made my way downstairs for breakfast. After Clyde, they had become almost like robots. They never spoke to me much. And I didn't speak to them, either. Sometimes we'd have small talk, but that was about it. I felt as if I was living with ghosts most of the time.

As I entered the kitchen, I realized they had both already left for work. I relaxed a little and eased back into the pantry, and stood there for a second. I felt like an intruder in someone else's house.

I'd eat dinner at Charlotte's house sometimes. She always complained about how her parents acted like kids. But I loved it. From her room, you could hear the sound of pots and pans hitting the kitchen floor and the chorus of her parents' laughter. Charlotte's mom was a terrible cook, and before every meal her dad would sneak into her room and tell all of us, "Now, I know it's going to suck but just grin and bear it because she worked really hard, okay?"

Charlotte would roll her eyes like always, clearly mortified, but Kia and I would just laugh and promise that we'd pretend that we loved it. And even though the meals weren't great, I loved dinner at Charlotte's, because there was noise. There was the sound of dishes clanking and food being served and conversation. And I imagined that even though she was an only child, she probably never felt like it.

Going to her house for dinner reminded me of what my family had once been like. Clyde and I would wake up to huge plates of pancakes and my dad would always turn on the news and make us come sit and watch it with him. And even though it was pretty boring, I was usually half asleep so I never really minded much about what was on. It was just nice to be with my father before he went to work. He and Clyde would talk about every sport under the alphabet and I'd dance around the kitchen, chatting with my mom and helping her do dishes. And as I fleeted back to my room, I thought about the fact that I never appreciated those mornings enough. They seemed like nothing back then, an almost boring routine, but now I'd do anything to get it back.

After I finished my breakfast, I started to pack up my clothes for camp. This time tomorrow, I'd be on a bus to a camp that was only an hour away, with a bunch of girls who had nothing in common with me. I wondered whether I'd sit with Kia and Charlotte or whether I'd have to be the awkward girl sitting in the back by herself. I was guessing the second one. I had enjoyed camp a lot when I was younger. Without it, I would have never met Kia. But as you get older, you start to question things, like the fact that faith might be bigger than just singing some songs and doing hand signals. Bigger than acting like the perfect Christian girl and constantly forcing a smile.

Though I didn't believe in wallowing in self-pity, I didn't exactly believe in putting on an act either. And that's what camp felt like. A ton of girls just trying to look better and more pure than the others. I could already hear their fake sympathetic tones as they grabbed me tightly. "Oh, Evelyn. I'm just so sorry about your brother."

I didn't want to hear it. And I didn't want to think about it anymore, either. I didn't even bother to grab my jacket or lock the door. I just left as fast as I possibly could. I climbed out of my window, legs shaky, arms tired.

I regretted not grabbing my jacket the minute I felt the freezing cold air bite at my exposed skin, but I kept on going, not caring enough to turn back. Five minutes later, it started pouring, and that's when I really regretted it. Still, I kept walking, hoping it would slow down and eventually stop.

Ten minutes later, it had picked up even more, but the bright yellow Cafe Soleil sign was clear even through the heavy rainfall. I burst through the door, absolutely soaked from the head down.

I expected to see Lorelei and feel relieved but when I walked up to the counter, there was a boy standing there, outwardly gawking at me. I'm sure I was gawking at him, too. A handful of people worked at Soleil, and I knew them all very well.

I had never seen this boy in my life.

The first thing I noticed was how tan he was, and that he looked about seventeen.

He didn't say a word; he just stared at me.

"Could I get an RJ please?" I said through chattering teeth.

I realized that was the first time I had ever had to tell someone my order since sixth grade. He just nodded once, and disappeared behind the coffee maker. I stood there, freezing, eager to have something warm.

He pushed it towards me without a word, and I handed him the exact change and walked straight to my usual table, still incredibly confused. I didn't even wait for my chai to cool down; I gulped a couple quick sips and winced as it burned at my tongue. I could still feel his eyes on me. I waited for him to look away, but he didn't.

And suddenly the whole course of the horrible day just hit me like a brick. I spun around in my chair to face him. "Can I help you or something?"

He blinked a couple of times, clearly taken aback, and after a few seconds he said, "whoa, sorry, chick."

Chick. All it took was one word for me to know he wasn't from here. He walked out from behind the counter, and I suddenly noticed how oddly he was dressed. He was wearing a short-sleeved shirt and board shorts. I was starting to believe I hadn't woken up from my dream.

"You know it's thirty degrees outside, right?" I said, nodding toward his shorts.

He laughed and walked closer to me. "Says the one who looks like she just got worked in a gnarly set."

"A what?" I asked, bewildered.

He opened his mouth as if he was about to explain and then closed it again. "Don't worry about it. Look, I didn't mean to freak you out; it's just I was losing it over there...I just can't get over how much you look like him."

I hesitated. "Who?"

He studied me for a moment. "Your brother."

"Clyde?" I was completely flustered. "Wait...you knew Clyde?"

"Knew him? He was like my own brother. He was my best friend."

The sense of admiration was so strong in his voice, I couldn't doubt it even if I wanted to.

But it didn't make any sense. I knew every single one of Clyde's friends here. I practically had spent as much time with them as he had.

"But I've never even seen you around here..." Then it suddenly dawned on me. "You're from that beach town he always went to..."

"What, Waverly?"

There was something so satisfying about hearing its name. "Yeah, Waverly."

He ran a hand through his tousled brown hair. "Really that obvious, huh?"

"Like a fish out of water."

"I was trying to keep it low-key."

More strange words.

"Well, you failed." I pressed, "Why are you here?"

A glint of playfulness sparkled in his eyes. "Funny you asked. I'm here for you."

He sat in the seat next to me, leaning back on it and watching my expression.

"Yeah, alright," I muttered, wondering why he couldn't just be honest with me. I examined him. I couldn't tell whether he was cute or not. He was the kind of exotic attractive type. No matter how cute he was, I wasn't about to sit here and be lied to.

"No, really." His tone was still light but serious. "Clyde had told me you wouldn't believe me at first but he also told me that I couldn't stop trying until I got you to."

I shot him a look. "Who are you, anyway?"

"Cyrus."

His name seemed oddly fitting.

"Okay, Cyrus." I was still feeling annoyed. "Enlighten me."

"This is pretty heavy but..." He leaned in, clasping his hands together. "The last time I saw him, he made me promise him something."

I tried to find some kind of dishonesty in his light green

eyes, but there was none. "Which was?"

"I promised him that if anything were to ever happen to him, I'd take you to Waverly for the summer. Get you out of this crazy place."

"C'mon, that's bullshit."

My annoyance suddenly hit an all-time high. Even talking about Clyde was off limits. This was too far.

He sighed, pinching the temple on his forehead. "I don't expect you to believe me."

"Why would he tell you that?" I confronted him. "He didn't even know the plane was going to crash."

He tossed his hands up in the air. "I really don't know..."

"Sick joke," I hissed as I went to stand. I was gripping my chai tea so tightly it easily could've exploded in my hands.

"Okay look, Evie." He reached forward and touched my arm lightly. "And yeah, I know not to call you Evelyn because you think it sounds old and boring." He made a face at my shocked expression. "A swell just hit back home and it's going off—huge, beautiful overhead sets. Eighty degree weather. Do you really think I came to this rainy kook-filled town to come on vacation? No. I'm here for you."

As crazy as it seemed, everything Cyrus had said made sense. Clyde *had* told me he'd get me to Waverly no matter what. And he had told me about his friends there, too. Cyrus fit the perfect description for one of them. I mean, how else would he know who I am? Or stupid things like how I don't like being called by my full name? Obviously Clyde had trusted him, so why couldn't I?

"I know this is strange. But after I heard about the plane crash, I knew I had to follow through with the promise. I didn't need karma to bite me in the ass, and I don't want to let him down either."

I was good at reading people. Great at it, in fact. There wasn't one weird feeling I was getting from Cyrus. Not one thing telling me no. Still, it seemed unrealistic. I was really sure I hadn't woken up from my dream now. Still, a little part of me wondered, could it be possible? I mean, it was happening, wasn't it? He was here. With a plan. I was practically halfway ready to leave. I couldn't help the excitement that sparked under my skin; it seemed unbelievable but it was happening. It was real.

I could get away. I could leave.

"One question...why didn't you just come to my house? Why were you waiting here?"

"My parents own this little shack," he said, proudly. "It was the weirdest thing. Your bro and I were out in the water when I met him. And turns out he always came here."

"Oh," I said. I could see now he had Lorelei's eyes. "Any more surprises?"

"Nah," he said, shaking his head. "Got any more questions?"

"Nope." I was still on my guard.

"Oh, wait, maybe one." I pressed, "If what you're saying is true...my friends could come, right?"

"Are you kidding me?" Cyrus's eyes went huge. "Of course, brah. Rule number one of surfers, don't go anywhere without your mates."

After talking to Cyrus for a while, he had left me his number and a plan to leave the next morning. I had just left the cafe when I felt my phone start to buzz in my pocket. I couldn't have been happier to see it was Kia.

"Just let me speak for a second," Kia rushed, the minute I answered. "I don't want to fight with you. I mean, it's so stupid. I'm not even angry with you or anything. And you were right, anyway; this whole plan to get out of here was stupid. We'll just go to camp like we always do and it'll be fun and—"

"No Kia, you were right," I interrupted.

"What?" Kia asked, surprised. "No, I'm not."

"You are! I don't even know how to explain what just happened but I just met one of Clyde's friends and he's taking us! We're leaving!'"

"Evie? Are you feeling okay?"

I couldn't control the excitement in my voice. "I'll be at your house in five. Tell Charlotte."

It had started raining again, but I didn't even take the time to regret that I hadn't brought my jacket.

FOUR

"Are you insane?"

I had just finished rambling out my plan to Charlotte and Kia. We were all crowding together in Charlotte's room. I almost laughed at their expressions. Kia's eyes were blank. And Charlotte was straight out gawking at me.

"Are you sure you feel alright?" Kia asked again, worried. "Did you get hit on your way here or something?"

I hadn't expected them to react normally. I had felt pretty confident about the plan in the cafe with Cyrus, but saying it out loud, I could hear how crazy it actually sounded. I didn't reply. I wasn't quite sure how I was going to convince them of what I had to say.

"So let me get this straight..." Charlotte gauged. "You want us to leave tomorrow morning to go to this beach town, God knows where, with this complete stranger that claims he knew your brother?"

Kia let out a deep breath. "Well, when you put it in that perspective..."

"Sounds fun," Charlotte chimed.

Kia glared at her. "No, no, this is not okay. Let's talk this over."

"Look, I know I just met this guy but it's not like I just straight up believed him. He knows things that only Clyde and I had talked about."

Kia was persistent. "Okay, so he knew Clyde. That doesn't make him a good person."

"But *Clyde* was a good person; he wouldn't just send some creep to come get his little sister. He'd send someone he trusted." I tried desperately to make my plan sound sane. In my head, it made perfect sense. It wasn't unlike Clyde to be thinking ahead of time and make abnormal promises.

"That's true...Clyde would never put us in a bad situation."

I could hear the softness in Kia's voice and I could tell she was starting to warm up to the idea.

Charlotte was up for anything. Danger was appealing to her. She had a smirk playing on her lips.

"There's a million reasons why this could go wrong."

Kia debated, "And one reason why it could go right."

"I know." I said, "That's why I understand if you guys don't want to...but I'm going."

"Well...." Kia muttered, "I'm definitely not letting you be this stupid by yourself."

"Really?" I was stunned. I couldn't hold back the thrill in my voice. "You guys will go?"

Charlotte winked. "There's no way I'm letting you lounge on the beach in a bikini all by your lonesome."

"Amen," Kia mumbled, but she was still a little hesitant. "But speaking of camp...we can't just not show up. They'd call our parents."

"Crap," I muttered. "I didn't think of that."

"Reason number one..." Kia mumbled under her breath.

"We can have Cyrus call them tomorrow. I mean...he sounds older. He could act like our dads or something."

"They might get suspicious," Kia countered. "But we might as well give it a try."

"And our parents will still be under the impression we're at camp?" Charlotte asked.

"Mhhmmm," I hummed. "We'll be back in a few weeks. The day camp ends."

"What about money?" Kia proceeded.

"I've got it covered, but speaking of that...I better go and get it all together."

Cyrus had told me that Clyde had left me money somewhere in his room. Where exactly, he didn't know. So it was my job to find it.

"Pack up tonight," I announced, "and be ready at six in the morning. We'll meet at Soleil and leave from there."

"Evie," Kia began as I started to leave. "Do you really think this is going to work?"

"I don't know," I answered honestly. "But I just have a good feeling about it, you know?"

Then suddenly Charlotte, Kia and I all looked at one another and screamed. We hugged goodbye and said we'd see each other bright and early.

I set my mind to work the minute I crawled back through my window. The first thing I needed to do was to find the money Clyde had hidden for me. His room was right near mine. I crept into the hallway and paused as I reached for the door handle. I hadn't gone in Clyde's room since he had died.

After a month of him being gone, my dad had walked through the hallway, his expression so cold and broken as he reached for my brother's door, and closed it in one swift movement. I think it was too painful to see it slightly open, waiting for his music to pour out or to listen for the scribble of his pen as he drew sketches of the surfboards he wanted. No one had opened it since. They had never found Clyde's body in the crash. We never really got much closure.

I turned it slowly, making sure not to make any noise. I closed my eyes and shut it painfully slow behind me. I felt around for the light switch and flicked it on; the light fluttered for a second and then the room was fully bright and I could see everything I had tried so hard to forget. The turquoise Converses he wore every day still by the door. His beachy hoodies hanging from the post of his bed. His sketches still sprawled across his desk where there should have been homework. All the surfing posters and pictures of girls in bikinis. You can tell a lot about a person by looking at their room.

Clyde was a guy from rainy Mokelumne Hill, but this was his sanctuary. Here, he dreamed of getting away. And he didn't just dream; he planned. I swallowed the lump in my throat and reminded myself that these were only things. I had to pretend this wasn't as hard as it was if I wanted to find what I was looking for. I thought of a good hiding spot, and my eyes instantly landed on his dresser. That's where most things were hidden in movies, always buried under a pile of clothes. I took his shirts out carefully, checked the pockets in his pants, even glanced around in his boxer drawer but there was nothing. I squeezed under his bed and looked for any kind of box but there were only some stray socks and his old broken ukulele. I checked his desk, around his TV, under his skateboards. But still, nothing.

Then, a logo caught my eye. It was a logo on one of his hats sitting on his nightstand. A red wave. I walked to it and picked it up slowly, turning it in my hands.

Underneath the hat sat a small wooden box. A smile spread across my face as I went to open it, but then faltered as I realized it was locked. I tried to think where he would keep a key. Where would I keep a key? I looked at the hat again and turned it over in my hands. There, taped to the top on the inside, was a little key. I smiled wide and inserted it into the lock, opening the box. Inside was cash, and lots of it. My eyes widened as I counted through hundreds of dollars. He didn't make much working at Soleil. He must've saved up for months to give me this, I thought.

I felt tears well in my eyes as I realized just how generous my brother was. He had kept his promise, even after he had died. I clutched the key in my hand, realizing it had been the object in my dream.

I put it safely into my pocket and held on to the little wooden box in my hands. I reached for his blue hoodie, knowing I had to take at least something of him with me. I was just about to open the door when I heard footsteps coming my way. My heart started racing as they came closer. I sat in the corner of the room, and hid the box behind me just in time.

"Evelyn? Are you in here?" my mother called from the other side of the door, bewildered. She stayed behind the door, not daring to step into his room.

"Come on out. This room is off limits, remember?"

I could hear heels click against the tile as she walked back down the hallway. I rested my head against the wall, blinking back tears.

My parents had been upset the first month or two Clyde was gone. My mother would cry. My father barely spoke. But still, they held me close. But after those two months, they became cold, frigid. Had they realized life was better without him? Without children at all maybe? Were they hoping I would somehow fall off the face of the planet too? I was never pretty enough to impress their lawyer and doctor friends. And Clyde was never smart enough.

I turned off the lights and closed the door. I hid the box

safely in my room and went out to the dining room to get dinner. My mother didn't say anything about me being in Clyde's room, and my father was watching the news. So it didn't matter much, anyway. I played with the food on my plate. I didn't have an appetite anymore. I couldn't tell whether it was from the sadness that hit me from being inside Clyde's room or the excitement of leaving in the morning.

I packed quickly, going through a checklist in my head of all the things I needed. I wasn't really sure what you would bring to the beach, because I hadn't been in so long. Obviously a bathing suit. I toyed with the pink frilly one I had dug up that was from at least two summers ago. I didn't even like pink anymore or have boobs back then. I shoved it in my suitcase, knowing it would have to do. It was late, and the excitement had worn off a little and now the stress was starting to sink in. I turned on the shower, and tried to calm my thoughts as I let the hot water run over me.

What if this didn't work? What if Cyrus ended up being a psycho killer and this was all just some evil trick? We were three teenage girls going to a place we had never been before, with no car. We were practically helpless. It was the most idiotic idea. It shouldn't have been taking up room in my head; it shouldn't have even been happening but it was. I thought back to those late-night mystery stories on the news and how the word "instinct" always played the biggest part. I closed my eyes and tried to listen for the feeling of this being wrong. That was all I needed to call this whole thing off. But the feeling never came.

Deep down, I was confident in this plan because I was confident in Clyde.

The clock read twelve a.m. when I finally felt as if I had finished everything. I climbed in my bed and scrolled through all the text messages Kia and Charlotte had sent me. Charlotte was clearly excited, and Kia was still on the fence about it all. I knew when she met Cyrus, she'd feel better about it. I tossed and turned in bed for a few hours. The excitement had caught up to me and now the worry had, too. Did I forget something? What if we couldn't get out of camp? What if our parents found out? For some reason, I just couldn't believe that this time tomorrow I'd be falling asleep to the sound of waves. So I pretended as if it were just any other night in the small town of Moke Hill. I pretended this is exactly where I'd be tomorrow night, too. I calmed my thoughts and told myself I wasn't leaving, until eventually I fell asleep.

FIVE

I awoke in a start, wondering why I hadn't woken up to the sound of my alarm. The first thing I did was check my phone. The alarm icon was still on the screen, meaning it hadn't even gone off yet. I still had twenty minutes before it was planned to wake me up at five thirty, but I knew I couldn't fall back asleep. I rubbed at my eyes. I still felt a little tired, and it took me a moment to realize why I had woken up so early anyway. I looked at all my packed bags by the door, and remembered I really was leaving today.

The anticipation started to sink in as I went to the kitchen and poured a cup of coffee. The smell of it filled my nostrils, and after a few sips, I already felt more awake. I wasn't hungry this early, so I went back to my room and put on the clothes I had set out last night, a pair of leggings and a long-sleeved shirt. Cyrus hadn't told me exactly where Waverly was, but he had said it was a six-hour car ride to Los Angeles and then we'd be close. There was no way I was dressing to impress. I twisted my dark blonde hair into a messy bun, washed my face, brushed my teeth, and for the hundredth time in my head, went through the list of everything I had brought.

Usually we left for camp around eight. So when my mom had come in last night to see how the packing was going, I had told her all of us girls were meeting early at Soleil for a leader meeting and then leaving from there.

~~

When I walked into the kitchen, my dad wasn't there, and I knew that meant he had already left for work. I felt a sharp pang, wondering why he couldn't have just stuck around a little bit longer to say goodbye. But I guess it didn't really matter.

My mom was leaning against the counter, watching the rain dribble down the window when I made my way downstairs. A cup of coffee was in one of her hands, and she had a faraway expression in her eyes. I wondered what she was thinking about. Did she miss Clyde? Did she want him to come back?

"I'm going to go now," I murmured, and even though my voice was low, I had startled her.

"Oh, Evelyn. I thought you were sleeping." She paused. "Do you have everything?"

"Yes. I triple checked."

"You're not in your uniform," she acknowledged, looking me over.

"I was just going to change at Soleil. I wouldn't want to get it dirty or anything," I replied.

"Oh, I suppose not," she agreed. She looked out the window again. "It's raining awfully hard. I'll take you."

"I'll be fine."

She slipped her feet into her slippers and grabbed her car

keys. "Don't be silly."

I shivered as soon as I stepped outside and I was grateful she had wanted to drive me. I had forgotten how cold Moke got in the early morning. My mom's Mercedes purred as we pulled out of the driveway. We were silent as we drove and I was glad Soleil was only five minutes away. I couldn't help but feel guilty even in those few minutes. My mom was completely under the impression of a lie, and although it wasn't harmful to her, I knew it wasn't right, either. I suppose most teenagers wouldn't have cared very much, but for some reason it made my stomach twist.

The sun just started to rise as we pulled up to Soleil. I could see one of the lights was turned on inside, and from where I was I could just make out a couple of figures.

"Have fun."

"Thanks, Mom."

She looked me in the eyes. "And be safe."

"It's church camp." I had to stifle a laugh. "But I will be."

I went to reach for the door and I felt her hand stop me. "I love you."

I froze, and I was glad I wasn't facing her so she couldn't see my expression. I hadn't heard those words in a while. They made me feel angry instead of happy. They made me feel cold instead of warm. They had said they loved Clyde. Night after night after night, but as soon as he had died, they acted as if they hardly cared at all. Like he didn't even exist. How could their "I

42

love you" be true, if it became removed as soon as he had gone?

"Goodbye," I said, closing the door.

I pulled my suitcase out of the car and watched her as she drove away. From the rearview mirror, I could've sworn I saw her crying, clutching the steering wheel with one hand, a tissue in the other.

My heart was aching so hard, I had to turn away before tears welled in my eyes, too.

I walked into Soleil to see Kia and Cyrus sitting at the table. Kia jumped up and gave me a hug as soon as she saw me, squealing in excitement.

"So you two have already met?" I asked Cyrus, who didn't look tired in the least.

"Yep. She got here even before I did."

She was obviously feeling more comfortable after she had talked to him.

"I couldn't sleep," Kia chimed. "Oh, and we called the camp. They totally believed Cyrus."

"Really?" I asked, surprised. "What'd you tell them?"

"We've come down with a horrible virus." Kia coughed, and then winked.

The bell on the door rang and Charlotte suddenly burst through, her freckled cheeks burning pink. "It's freaking freezing," she said through chattering teeth, pulling her oversized

Nirvana sweatshirt tighter around her.

"Here." Kia pushed a cup of coffee towards her. Charlotte eagerly started gulping it down.

"So you're the strange guy...." Charlotte accused Cyrus as soon as she had finished. She lifted her eyebrow as she looked him over.

"Cyrus," he replied, seeing she obviously was looking for something wrong with him. "Would you like to pat me down?"

"Are you trying to get me to touch you?"

Cyrus practically started choking on his coffee. "What? No!"

"Sure. Huh." Charlotte mused. She stuck out her hand. "You brought your record, right?"

Cyrus looked appalled. "Why would I—"

"Trick question," Charlotte interrupted. "So you do have a record..."

"Charlotte!" Kia said in astonishment. "He's just a boy!"

"My point exactly. Boys are evil."

She eyed Cyrus once more and then strutted off towards the coffee counter.

"I'm sorry," I told Cyrus, who still looked a little flustered. "That's Charlotte for you."

"Yeah, she's a handful alright." He laughed. "We should

probably get on the road. Would hate to get stuck in traffic."

Cyrus led us out back to the alley and there was only one car parked there. All three of us looked at one another, at Cyrus, and then back at the car. The car looked like something from a movie, a turquoise colored Volkswagen van. Clearly old, the bright paint masked a lot of the little dings. I was starting to think the family had a thing for eccentric paint jobs.

Kia crinkled her nose with a smile. "I like her."

"Well, I know she's nothing fancy, but she's my girl." Cyrus admired her once more, and then pulled the door open for us. "You gals coming?"

"Just so you know, I'm a black belt," I heard Charlotte tell Cyrus. "So consider yourself warned."

Kia and I couldn't stop laughing as she climbed in after us.

The inside of the van was exactly what you'd expect it to be. Sand covered the carpet and the schoolbus-styled seats. There were scattered board shorts and random t-shirts, jugs of water, towels, and surf magazines.

"Just throw your bags in the back," Cyrus called as he played with the radio. He reached for a CD that read "The Dirty Heads" and a fast beat filled the car.

"What's this?" Charlotte asked, holding up a piece of something that looked like a bar of soap.

Cyrus's eyes widened at her question. "Surfboard wax...."

"Oh," she replied, bringing it up to her nose. "It smells delicious."

Cyrus just chuckled and pulled out of the alley. The car moved smoothly down the road.

Charlotte grabbed my hand suddenly and, with a smile, squeezed it.

"We're really leaving," Kia said in disbelief.

The music was turning my insides, making everything feel knotted. I was overwhelmed by the sudden excitement that came over me as Kia's words settled into my head. Six hours from now and I'd be in a place I had only ever dreamed about. I wondered whether Clyde knew his promise would be kept. I pressed my hand against the cold glass window, watching the rain dribble down, watching as Mokelumne Hill disappeared far behind me.

SIX

"Evie, wake up."

I heard the voice, but I was too comfortable. I kept my eyes shut, drifting between sleep and awake.

"Maybe we should just pour water on her."

"That's rude."

"Well, at this rate she could be dead."

"Evie." It was Kia's voice again. "We're here."

Those words were all I needed to pull me out of my deep sleep. I opened my eyes and they instantly burned from the light coming through the window. I squeezed them shut hard, and after a moment, I hesitantly opened them again.

"Finally, Sleeping Beauty has awoken," Cyrus announced.

I yawned and started to sit up; immediately my neck started feeling tight. I worked the kinks out with my hand, making a mental note to bring a pillow next time.

"I need coffee," I groaned.

"No. What you need is to look out the window," Kia chirped.

I risked a glance out the window again, my eyes adjusted better to the brightness this time, and after a moment of squinting, the scene outside became clear. I was suddenly pushed into a completely different world. At least it felt like it. I stared in awe as the sun glistened along the ocean, the perfect shade of blue kissing the long sandy beach that surrounded the never-ending pier. I stuck my hand out the window, the sun hot against my arm, leaving the skin where it touched feeling tingly and new.

We came to a stoplight, and a huge crowd of people started to make their way across the crosswalk. Everywhere you looked was bare skin. Shirtless, tanned boys. Blonde girls in barely-there bikinis. The sound of waves fell softly, with the loud chatter of people turning the mixed sounds into a soundtrack of summer. The blur of people seemed to go on forever before the light turned green.

We turned onto another road, heading away from the ocean.

"This is Main Street," Cyrus said.

Main Street, like the pier, was flooded with people. A few small kids suddenly ran in front of our car, surfboards tucked under their arms. Cyrus hit the brakes fast, barely missing one of the bronzed young boys.

"Watch yourself, groms!" Cyrus called out the window.

They laughed and kept running towards a big surf shop that was directly across from the pier. All of Main Street was lined up with small shops and stores. There were so many, I didn't have enough time to catch all of their names, but from what I could see, they all looked like a mix between surf shops, bars, and ice cream diners. I realized I had never imagined a place like this. Not even my dream had been able to capture a place such as this. Clyde hadn't been over exaggerating when he had said there were no words to describe it. I wondered how many times he had walked Main Street. I wondered what stores he had been in and which were his favorite. I didn't feel sad when I thought about Clyde here. Only excited.

"This is amazing," Charlotte gasped.

Kia was still silent, staring out the window in awe just as I had been, a heavy admiration in her eyes.

"I can't believe we're here."

"Neither can I," Kia finally answered.

We turned left onto another street, making our way through the neighborhood. The crowds of people had diminished, and it suddenly became quiet. Waverly couldn't have been more different from Moke Hill. Unlike Moke, where we had land far and wide, the houses in Waverly were all extremely close to one another. Some were elegant and tall, some were dainty and cute, some looked beat-up, with surfboards lying on the front lawn. I started to notice Waverly didn't really have a pattern. They didn't have a rich side and a poor side. Next to a multimillion dollar home, you'd see an older beach shack. And there was something so refreshing about that. Suddenly, Cyrus stopped at the end of the street, in front of a little rickety house.

"Well, here we are, girls."

We all leapt out of the car as fast as we could, eager to be outside in the ocean air. I winced as I hopped out of the van. I hadn't expected to be so sore from the long drive. The six hours had definitely been worth it, though. Cyrus came over and helped us get our bags out. Then he went back, grabbing a surfboard from his car.

Charlotte had already started to make her way up the steps to the shack when Cyrus stopped her.

"What are you doing?" Cyrus called, as he locked up the van.

"What? Did you want us to sleep outside or something?" Charlotte muttered.

"No. But if you want to sleep on my neighbor's lawn that's cool, too."

"Isn't this your house?" Kia asked.

"No." Cyrus laughed; he pointed a finger to one that was a couple of houses down. Charlotte's eyes widened as we walked towards it. A tall, skinny house, it was a little bit more narrow than the other big ones. It was definitely the prettiest house on the block, with a brand new yellow paint job and brown accents.

"I think he's lying to us," Charlotte said, as she approached the door.

"Oh yeah?" Cyrus moved around us, still holding his surfboard and shoved the key into the door, pushing it open.

"Welcome home."

"Wow," Kia said as soon as we had walked in.

The door opened up to a roomy living room, with dark wooden floors, an oversized TV, and a fireplace. The couch was huge, and the minute we had walked in, Cyrus had gone over and put his surfboard on it. The living room was back to back with a pretty kitchen with marble tops and pictures everywhere. Cyrus led us up the stairs. It opened up to another small little hangout place with couches and chairs and then split off into two separate hallways.

"This is my brothers' room. That is, when they come back home," he said, knocking on the first door we approached. It had a sign on it that read, "Erik and Neils."

"This is my room," he said at the next door, which was covered in stickers of surf and skate brands. "Bathroom," at the one after that.

We went back down the hallway, past the living room, where there was only a set of double doors. "This is my aunt's room. You'll meet her tonight."

Right by her room was another flight of stairs. My arms burned already from carrying my bags, but we followed him up eagerly.

"And this..." he announced, as we rounded the corner, "is your room."

The first thing I noticed was two glass doors leading out to the balcony straight ahead. The room took up the whole third story. Three queen size beds were covered with pretty Hawaiian comforters. The rest of the room was filled with nightstands, huge dressers, a TV, tall windows, a couple chairs decorated with colored pillows, and a door clearly leading to a bathroom.

"This is perfect," Kia admitted, falling back onto one of the beds.

"Seriously," Charlotte added.

"It is," I agreed, turning back to Cyrus. "Thank you."

Cyrus half smiled and gave a shrug of his shoulders. "It's no big deal. I'm glad we made it. To be honest, I wasn't sure my old girl could truck it all the way to Moke and back."

I felt a new appreciation for the little bright van, and I was glad she had stuck it out. "Well, she did."

"That's right." He nodded. "Well, why don't you girls hurry and unpack? You all have got places to go and people to meet."

SEVEN

One day I had been sitting with Clyde in Soleil, right before he had died, and I had asked him to explain what Waverly was like. It was one of the only times I had asked him about it, because he had told me he couldn't really explain. I usually kept my mouth closed, but I had been staring out the window, trying to grasp any thought that would let me get lost for a little while. And I wanted so desperately to know.

And so I asked him, "What are the people like?"

I was sure that even if he couldn't explain the place, he could at least explain the people that lived there. He had taken a sip of his black coffee, which I always found revolting, and closed his eyes for a moment as if he were trying to picture one of them.

"Do you remember Disneyland?" he asked me, after he had opened them.

"Kind of." I shrugged, not knowing what Disneyland had anything to do with my question. "I was only ten. That was a long time ago."

"Well, it's kind of like that," he mused. "There are people from all over the world that go there. I guess it's funny, how they all come from different places and they're all looking for the same thing."

I could see a hint of sadness in Clyde's eyes when he spoke about Waverly. I could tell that he missed it.

As I walked with Cyrus, Charlotte, and Kia through Main Street, our conversation knocked around inside my head. *Disneyland.* I looked around at the crowds of people that surrounded us, and it was true. Some were very obviously foreigners, their accents being heard quickly over the gush of other sounds. Some were still dressed as if they were back home in the snow, and others were clearly locals, with their dark tans and worn bikinis and board shorts. I still was noticing a lot of skin.

"Hey Cy!"

I heard the sound of a skateboard, and suddenly Kia squealed and jumped out of the way as it almost ran into her. The boy turned around quickly and came skating back, a worried expression on his face.

"Sorry 'bout that," he told Kia. "Did I get you?"

"No. I'm fine."

Kia's voice got twice as high as normal and I could tell she thought he was cute. He was Kia's taste, too: big dark eyes, tan skin, black spiky hair. There was something very soft about him.

"That was a good first impression." Cyrus chuckled, slapping the boy hard on the back.

The boy ignored him and stuck his hand out to Kia. "Hi. I'm Noah."

He shook hands with Charlotte and then stopped as he reached for mine. "I'm sorry to hear about your brother. He was a really cool guy."

His eyes became so warm and kind, I was scared he might start crying. "Thank you."

He nodded once kindly and then picked his skateboard back up. "Where you guys off to?"

"Swells."

"When Mave is working? Jeez, are you trying to scare the poor girls away?"

"That's why they have me as their bodyguard."

"You better let him know these girls are off limits," Noah demanded.

"Don't worry," Cyrus reassured him. "He already does."

Noah glanced at his watch quickly. "Well, I gotta go. Bye, guys."

He smiled shyly and then jumped back on his skateboard, quickly disappearing into the cluster of people.

Charlotte and I both bumped into Kia as we kept making our way down Main. She kept her eyes on the ground, the cheesiest smile on her face.

It wasn't just the sounds that made up Main Street; it was the smells, too. The smell of Mexican food and alcohol floated through the street. Occasionally, the smell of Hawaiian food and barbecue leaked in. Then suddenly, as we passed a gelato parlor, the air was overtaken with sweetness, almost begging you to come inside the shop and taste some. My stomach grumbled but we all pushed past the area and started to walk towards the surf shop I had seen earlier from the car, the one on the corner, right across from the pier. A crowd of people lingered outside the door near the "Rent Surfboards Here" sign.

"I'm going to introduce you guys to some of my pro friends."

I felt my hands start to get sweaty. *Pro friends*? As in *pro* surfers. Here in Waverly, meeting pro surfers was most likely the equivalent to meeting a celebrity in Hollywood. For some reason, it made me feel super nervous.

"No...no...it's okay."

Cyrus raised his eyebrow at me. "Why not?"

"Why don't we head to the pier?" I suggested, avoiding his question.

"Nope. We're going in. C'mon!"

Before I had time to argue, Cyrus plunged his way into the crowd. He made his way through the obnoxious gathering easily, while Kia, Charlotte, and I had a bit harder of a time.

"Excuse me," I mumbled over and over again as I pushed through the half-naked mass. All I could see was skin, bikinis, long hair, and snapbacks. A few boys smirked at me as I rubbed past them. I tried my best to not grind against anyone's practically naked boyfriend as I squeezed myself through. The last thing I needed was to be confronted by some temperamental blonde. I was starting to think my idea to go to the pier was much better than this.

I let out a sigh of relief as I finally made it into the shop. Even then, there was still a crazy amount of people. At least I could manage to walk without feeling as if I was on top of someone. I was grateful for that.

Swells was slightly hard to make out due to the amount of people in it, but from what I could see, it was quite big. Surfboards of all different shapes and sizes lined the whole left side of the surf shop. Some were smaller than me, with pointed noses and pulled-in tails. Others were wider shaped, the nose smooth and rounded. The few longboards here and there were hard to miss with their eccentric colors and vivid designs. But for the most part, it seemed to be mainly performance boards.

To the right was a long counter. Behind it, there held all different kinds of stuff for surfing. Fins, stickers for your boards, wetsuit cleaner, surf magazines. A man's head suddenly popped out from behind the counter. He looked startled at first when he saw Cyrus. "Back already, Cyrus? I thought it'd be a couple of days."

"I couldn't wait. I heard about the swell and I left as fast as I could."

The man chuckled. "I'm afraid you missed most of it. Last couple days have been gorgeous, though."

I studied the man. From far away, you would have never been able to tell he was older. He was still built as if he was young: tall and well-muscled. Long dark blonde hair that was just starting to get a tint of gray. There were wrinkles around his mouth and his eyes when he smiled. Not the same kind of wrinkles stressed-out people get from sitting in an office all day. These were the kind of wrinkles that said he had spent every waking moment he could in the sun, and he enjoyed every minute of it.

Cyrus introduced us to the man, whose name was John. The first question he asked us was whether we had ever surfed before. He didn't look surprised when we said no. He only told us that Cyrus would teach us and he wouldn't let us leave Waverly until we knew how.

After talking to John for a while, we made our way through the rest of the shop. The crowd cleared a little bit, and there in the middle of the room was a boy. Blonde, tall, tan. He had a surfboard laid flat on a stand and he was studying it. He looked focused, and even though there was a crowd surrounding him, he looked alone, too.

"Maverick," Cyrus called out to the boy as he made his way towards him. He gestured with his hand for us to come over there with him. Kia tapped my arm lightly and as soon as she got my attention, she made those eyes. Those "Isn't he a cutie?" eyes. I just laughed and ignored her. The boy, Maverick, watched us as we walked to him, his head cocked to the side. One hand cuffed around his neck; his other hand stayed on the board.

"Ladies. This is Maverick Greyson," Cyrus introduced us.

"And Maverick, this is Kia, Charlotte, and Evelyn."

Maverick brushed his eyes quickly over all of us, pausing on me a little bit longer than I liked. "It's a pleasure, girls."

His voice was somewhat friendly, with a hint of sarcasm leaking into it. The surf shop combined with a clothing store, and where we were standing was right where they crossed. A few girls caught sight of Maverick as they were walking out of the store and started to giggle. If he noticed, he didn't make any fuss about it. When I looked back towards him, he was still staring at me.

"You know, Maverick rips. One of the best groms in the world right now." Cyrus's eyes suddenly darted to a Nationals surfing contest program he had given us earlier. "I'd have him sign that for you, actually."

Maverick reached for Kia and Charlotte's program first, pulling a black marker out of his pocket. He signed it in one quick movement, and then handed it back with a charming smile. He reached for mine, and I gave it to him reluctantly. He clearly did this sort of thing a lot. He acted as if he were doing us a favor. He took a little longer to sign mine. I looked away as he did it, not wanting to give him any satisfaction. When he was done, I shoved it into Kia's bag without looking at it.

As if on cue, the giggling group of fifteen-year-old girls came around a second time. They lingered near the surfboard section closest to us, touching the boards and mumbling about them. It was pretty obvious they didn't know anything about surfing and they were only hovering in the section because of Maverick.

"Can we take a picture with you?" One of the girls looked up at Maverick, batting her eyelashes at him. She was the more confident one out of the four of them, and she was pretty, too. The rest of the girls laughed and re-adjusted their boobs in their push-up tops.

"Anything for a natural beauty like you," he said, smoothly. The girl looked as if she suddenly felt dizzy. Her friends all exchanged looks, clearly jealous.

"I'd like to test that 'natural beauty' statement with a makeup wipe," Charlotte muttered.

After he took the picture with them, he went on flirting, and eventually he came back to us, but not until after he gave them his number first.

"Wow. Four girls in ten minutes. Must be nice." Cyrus groaned. "Get ready for your phone to blow up."

Maverick shook his head, a smirk playing on his lips. "I didn't give them mine."

"Seriously, dude?" Cyrus looked annoyed with him. "You always do that shit. Why?"

"No challenge. They probably would've started stripping for me if the shop had been empty."

I felt immediately annoyed at his cockiness. Sure, the girls must get irritating, but he had completely put those girls under the impression that he liked them.

"Then why did you waste your time flirting with them?"

The question left my mouth so fast I had no time to recover. I hadn't meant to say anything, but there it was. My words hung awkwardly in the silence for a moment. Maverick eyed me, clearly surprised I had said them. He didn't let the shock linger on his face for too long; he composed himself in an instant.

"If you're good at the game than why not play?"

I didn't hesitate. "One day you're going to meet a girl who can play better than you."

Suddenly, he reached across the surfboard; his fingers brushed against my hand ever so lightly. I felt a jolt, and as much as I wanted to pull away from him, I couldn't. His hand fell back to his surfboard, and even though it only lasted for a second, it burned where his skin had just touched mine.

"Maybe when hell freezes over." He leaned in so close his face was a breath away from mine. He smelled like a mixture of salt water and cologne. "Twice."

I was usually good at being a smart-ass, but I immediately felt my cheeks get warm, my witty comeback get stuck in my throat. He stood there, so close, mouth twisted in a smirk, his eyes practically simmering.

"Let's go get some coffee," Kia interrupted, pulling at my arm.

It took me a second to register, but after a moment, I nodded and followed her towards the door. There was a coffee shop right next to Swells.

"What happened back there?" Kia asked me as soon as we were outside. "You got all...nervous and weird."

"I have no idea," I admitted.

She studied my face, and tried to hold back a laugh. "Looks like you've met your match."

I almost hesitated to keep the door open for her as we walked into the coffee shop. It was a tiny little place called Kae's Point.

"He thinks he's so cool," I rambled. "He's not even that hot."

Kia raised her eyebrow at me. "He's hands down an eleven out of ten."

The girl at the coffee counter kept smiling up at Kia and me as we waited in line. When we got to the front, she looked as if she wanted to say something, but she refrained.

I ordered two vanilla coffees and turned back to Kia. "That doesn't even make sense."

Kia crossed her arms over her chest, and gave a shrug. "All I know is I've never seen you blush that hard. Ever. Not even when freaking Colby Reagen wanted to hook up with you last week."

I shot her a glare. "Shut up."

Kia twirled a piece of her hair and made a face. "Someone has a crush."

"Kia, if you know what's good for you, you'll stop talking."

After we had gotten our coffee, we made our way back to Swells. But this time I lingered closer to the counter instead of the board section. I dared a glance over at Maverick again. His eyes were back on his board, his hand moving in circles as he waxed it. Kia was crazy if she thought I had a crush on him. He looked like any other stupid boy here. With his stupid blue eyes and his stupid tan skin. Waxing his stupid surfboard. So what if he had caught me off guard? That didn't mean anything. His eyes suddenly flickered to mine, a smile playing on his lips, and I felt words catch in my throat again. I didn't like the feeling, so I quickly looked away.

We left Swells shortly after, and I was relieved that I had made it out without having to speak another word to Maverick. Cyrus took us into a couple other surf shops that were much smaller but still looked the same. They even held the same sort of rambunctious surfer boys. We were introduced to even more people, and I was already unsure whether I could remember them all. By the time we left the last place and started to walk back to Cyrus's house, it was already dark outside. In Moke Hill, when nighttime hit, the only source of light came from the moon. But Main Street was draped in bright white lights that illuminated the whole street. It was never truly dark. I let the new taste of the warm vanilla coffee melt in my mouth as I watched the glow from the lights settle on the pavement and make it sparkle. The closer we got to the house, the more the sounds of the drunken people at the bars faded. Eventually, all you could hear was the sound of the waves crashing. I stopped walking for a second, closed my eyes, and just listened.

This place didn't feel real. Just a day earlier, I had been listening to the same droning sound of rain I had been for years. And now, I was here, the ocean practically my neighbor, feeling the warm night breeze softly touch my skin. I followed Cyrus, Charlotte, and Kia into the house but I half expected it to crumble down around us, proving to me this was just another daydream.

The smell of food abruptly broke into my thoughts.

"Thank God," Cyrus practically yelped as we rounded the corner of the hallway.

A tall, pale lady stood in the middle of the kitchen, carrying a bowl of bread rolls.

"Actually, my name's Auntie Tina. Obviously you're starving."

Her blue eyes suddenly widened as soon as she saw us. "Holy cats! You weren't lying!"

"Nope," Cyrus somehow got out, though I don't know how. He was practically shoving the bread rolls down his throat.

The hundreds of bracelets the woman had on jingled as she pulled us all in for a hug. "Oh, I'm so delighted you girls are here!"

She reached around and tore the bread bowl back out of Cyrus's hands. "Where are your manners?"

"We're so hungry," Charlotte admitted.

"Oh, wonderful!" She danced to the counter, where there was literally a buffet waiting for us. "Help yourselves. Mondays are Hawaiian nights. Kahlua pork. Sticky rice. Hilo beef. Macaroni salad."

She looked as though she couldn't contain herself; she was ecstatic as we all piled up our plates. We all made our way to the kitchen table as fast as we could, our stomachs growling. I had never had Hawaiian food but I didn't hesitate to shove a huge forkful into my mouth. I swear, it's one of the best feelings in the world—your first bite of a meal when you're starving. The food was delicious, though I couldn't tell whether it was because I was so hungry or whether it was actually really good.

"Thank you, Tina," I said, as soon as I was full enough to talk.

"It's Auntie Tina." She corrected me with a smile. "I was so excited when Cyrus told me you girls were coming. I mean, let's be honest, who wants a teenage boy around all the time?"

"Damn, Auntie, I didn't know you felt that way."

Kia started laughing from across the table. "Looks like we'll be moving in."

"You can go live in the van," Charlotte added, winking at Cyrus.

"Oh there's so many things we have to do! You all like clothes, right?" she asked.

"Of course," Charlotte blurted. "We might be from the

middle of nowhere but we *are* girls."

"Perfect!" Auntie Tina squealed. "I own a clothing shop just downtown. We'll go on a shopping trip tomorrow, get you looking like locals instead of some aliens."

"We're a little tight on money," Kia admitted.

"Money?" Auntie Tina's eyes grew wide. "Oh no, no, no. As long as you're with me, you don't worry your pretty little heads about paying a dime for anything."

Kia and Charlotte both suddenly stopped chewing their food and looked at me. We had Clyde's money, but he had only had one person in mind when he was saving that up. And we had a little money Charlotte and Kia had been able to scrounge together. I honestly wasn't sure how long it would last for all three of us. But I was determined to make it work.

"That's so generous, really," I answered. "But we can't do that."

"Yes we can," Charlotte muttered under her breath. I heard Kia kick her under the table.

"As long as you're here, I will treat you as if you were my own daughters," Auntie Tina said, her features suddenly turning serious. "And that means you're getting spoiled. Whether you like it or not."

"Damn it," Cyrus groaned, resting his head on the table. "What did I get myself into?"

After dinner, Charlotte, Kia, and I all said our goodnights, changed into our pajamas and climbed into our beds. Charlotte had left the balcony door open. I pulled the comforter tighter around me as the cool breeze flowed through the room. The sound of the ocean started to lull me to sleep, and just before I fell into unconsciousness, I prayed that I would be here when I woke up.

EIGHT

I was almost afraid to open my eyes when I awoke. I desperately didn't want yesterday to have been nothing but a dream. I didn't know what I'd do if it had been. But I could feel the warmth of the sun on my cheek, and again, the cool breeze from the ocean, and so I dared to open them. My eyes met a pair of crazy green ones instantly.

"Morning!"

"Oh my—" I yelled, startled. "Charlotte, what the hell?"

"I just said good morning!" Charlotte somehow got out in her fit of laughter.

"Most people say good morning, by, oh, I don't know, bringing someone a cup of coffee or breakfast in bed. Not standing over someone, staring at them!"

The bathroom door opened and suddenly Kia appeared, wearing a cute sundress and a towel wrapped around her head. "What happened?"

"Charlotte just freaked me out."

Charlotte had somehow ended up on the floor and was still laughing.

"Oh..." Kia trailed off. "Well, I believe breakfast is ready downstairs. Care to join me?"

Charlotte finally pulled herself back together and we all bounced downstairs towards the smell of bacon and pancakes.

"Good morning, good morning!" Tina sang. She was hovering over the stove, flipping another pancake, even though I swear there was a stack of about fifty right beside her.

"This smells delicious," Kia chirped.

"Thank you, dear. Why don't you get out the orange juice? It's just in the fridge to your left there," Tina answered, pointing to it.

I stood there in the middle of the kitchen for a second, just taking it all in. It was almost overwhelming. I was so used to waking up to a house that seemed vacant, as if I were living with ghosts. To hear cheery voices and to have the smell of bacon fill your nostrils and the promise of a good day—there just isn't anything in the world like it.

Charlotte looked around, a curious look on her face. "Where's Cyrus?"

As if to answer her question, we heard a loud set of steps bounding down the stairs, none other than a boy's. Everyone became silent as he came into view, reaching the last few steps.

Cyrus looked like an idiot. Standing there half asleep, in nothing but boxers. He looked himself over, still completely oblivious, and then his eyes met ours and it hit him.

"Oh, I guess I have to wear clothes now." He shrugged.

All of a sudden, a pancake came flying over my head, smacking Cyrus right on the cheek.

"Go on," Tina urged him, stifling a laugh.

"Okay, okay, I'm going." He reached down and picked the pancake off the floor, taking a big bite out of it as he made his way back up the steps.

"Boys." She rolled her eyes. "I hope he didn't ruin your appetite."

"Ruin?" Charlotte whispered to Kia and me. "Did you see those abs?"

"Charlotte," Kia shot. "Ew."

"What? I'm just saying."

After Cyrus had come downstairs again, actually dressed this time, we ate breakfast. I realized why Tina had made so much food. I had forgotten just how much a boy could eat. I also realized the food hadn't just tasted good last night because I was starving. It actually was good. *Really* good.

Kia was an early bird and Cyrus was a boy, so they were all set to leave. Charlotte and I headed upstairs to get ready for the day. After digging out my toiletries and spending at least ten minutes trying to figure out how to turn on the shower, I finally climbed into the warm water. I usually took my time in the shower. But as I massaged the strawberry-scented shampoo through my hair, I couldn't contain my excitement. I just wanted to be dressed and out the door as fast as possible. I toweled off my hair and left it to air dry, and quickly picked through my suitcase until I came across a pair of shorts and a simple black tank top. I wasn't about to care what I looked like. I just wanted to go explore already. I took my camera out of the camera bag carefully and hung it around my neck.

"Let's go," I hollered at Charlotte, who was putting on her third coat of mascara.

When we met Cyrus outside, he was standing there in a wetsuit, holding a short board. "Hey ladies, I hope you don't mind if I go surf for a little. You all can hang out on the pier and watch."

"Not at all," I said. "After you."

I expected when we started walking that I would finally be able to settle down. But I only grew more excited as we got closer to Main Street. It was still crowded downtown, but not as bad as it had been last night. The street mainly was overtaken by surfers. Bands of them. A couple every few minutes would run a cross the crowded roads to get to the surf. Sometimes people honked and cursed something at them. But for the most part everyone was cool about it. Most of the guys they were running in front of had boards loaded up in their cars; clearly they understood. There was a language that surfers had. No harm, no foul. I snapped a few pictures of the little scene, and kept walking. As we passed Swells, I noticed the girl who had been working at Kae's yesterday was watching me. She smiled kindly and then quickly looked away. I wondered why she had taken such a liking to us. I figured maybe she was just shy.

We joined the huge mass that was waiting to cross the crosswalk; most of the people had beach bags slung around their shoulders, or volleyballs in their hands, smelling of sweat and sunscreen. As the light turned green, we all made our way across in one big movement; the pier loomed straight ahead.

"I'm going that way," Cyrus said to us after we had crossed the street. He pointed to the stairs just by the side of the pier, leading down to the beach. "The view's better from the pier; you guys can watch for a bit. Then head down to the beach when you see me paddling in."

Before we could answer him, he was already being swept up with a group of other surfers who clearly knew him. They all raced across the sand, as if the waves would suddenly stop if they didn't get out there right away. As I watched, I imagined the water had a pull on all the surfers. Maybe that's why they'd run across busy roads, and push through crowds of people. Maybe that's why they didn't walk calmly down Main to get to the ocean—they ran as fast as they could, barely skimming people with the nose of their boards. The closest thing I could compare it with was music, the way music pulls on certain strings in you. When a good song comes on, and you can't help but to sing to it, or to dance. The water can do that, too.

As we walked down the pier, I tried to take in everything around me. Young musicians huddled around a bench, tapping drums, and strumming guitars with their guitar cases open, begging for any spare change. Photographers stood in the middle of the walkway, kneeling, trying to get the perfect angle for a shot. Farther down, you could make out the outline of fishermen, casting their fishing poles off the end of the pier. Kites were tied to the kite shops, dancing and fluttering in the wind. We walked into some of the shops that held all different kinds of little treasures. When we had finished shopping, we found a bench midway through our walk down the pier, and decided to watch Cyrus surf.

There is nothing like seeing the ocean from above. The ocean and the beach looked as if it were never-ending. From the beach, you can't really see the way it works. Everything is so close, so right in your face. But from above, you can start to see its rhythm. You can see a wave forming at its earliest stage, just the water starting to slowly build. Then you watch as it starts to form, and become a wave. At that point, that's when the surfers can see it. It's almost like a game: you can see a wave forming before they can, and you wonder who will catch it.

The surfers merely looked like game pieces in the water. They were everywhere. Where there was a wave, there were at least three people surfing it.

Kia blinked a few times at the water. "Umm...which one's him?"

Charlotte rolled her eyes at Kia and pointed down to a figure in the water. "That one. Obviously."

I studied it for a moment. Brown hair. Black wetsuit. Tan. Tiny board. "I think she's right."

Suddenly, he was on a wave, coming right towards us.

"Wow." Kia breathed, leaning over the railing to get a better look.

Then, in an instant, the wave abruptly closed in on him. His board went flying into the air, and a second later, he popped back up, his face much more noticeable now.

"That's not him." Kia squinted. "That guy is at least fifty."

"No, no, I swear it's him," Charlotte said, leaning over the railing. "Oh...okay, maybe not."

This happened at least ten more times, until we finally gave up on trying to find him. I realized it was pretty much impossible. They all looked the same out there.

The sun hit the water just perfectly, making the water glisten. I watched a wave starting to form. A tiny thing, really. Just water, slowly building. All the other surfers were looking past it, not paying any attention to it. Then, one surfer, one out of the fifty that were sitting there waiting for the perfect wave, started to paddle for it. I couldn't see the expressions on the others' faces, but they were all watching the one surfer, and I'm sure they were wondering why he was wasting his time. But from up above, I could see the wave building perfectly. Just as the wave formed into a beautiful peak, he dropped in on his board, straight down towards the bottom of the wave. He turned his board right before the wave had a chance to pick him up. Then the wave was curling over him; he was right there in the middle, just a second faster than the wave. I saw the boy reach his hand out and touch the water surrounding him. And I swear, my heart had stopped. I quickly lifted my camera up and snapped a picture of the moment. I wanted to trade places with him right then. I'd do anything to be in that wave. To feel what it was like. As the wave closed in, he kicked his board out, just skimming over the top of it, landing him right by the pier. All of a sudden, people started whistling and pumping their fists as the boy smiled back at them.

"Did you see that?" I asked, breathlessly.

"See what?" Kia and Charlotte answered in union.

I turned back around and pointed to the boy, up close now. I could see he was blonde, tan; he looked tall. And his wetsuit was different from most of the other boys—black and white, with just a hint of red.

"That wave he just caught."

"No," Charlotte admitted. "But damn, from up here he looks pretty good."

We couldn't find Cyrus out in the water, so we figured he was already done and decided to head down to the beach. We had only really seen it from the car when we had arrived. So, Charlotte, Kia, and I all eagerly pushed through the crowds of people surrounding the stairs. I kicked off my Converses and held them in my hand. My feet burned as I stepped onto the hot sand, but I didn't step back onto the cool pavement. This was a good kind of burn. The kind of burn I had been waiting for.

Getting across the first part of the beach was much like a war zone. One word: volleyball. The whole first section of the beach was lined with volleyball nets, with very competitive players, mostly shirtless boys. Meaning, they didn't care where you were. If the ball was coming your way, you better move.

"Jeez, could they at least put some clothes on?" Charlotte

muttered, as a ball went flying over her head. "It's like they want you to be distracted by how hot they are, so you stand there like an idiot and then get hit."

Even Kia, who was the good girl, gawked at the boys. It was kind of impossible. Hot, sweaty, boys. I mean, let's be honest, how could you not?

A couple of the boys yelled some foolish flirty thing that I didn't even bother to try to understand.

Charlotte, of course, smiled and looked around for whoever had said it.

"Thank gosh," Kia panted, as soon as we had passed them. "I thought I was going to die back there."

"That was practically heaven," Charlotte said, dreamily.

Kia and I just rolled our eyes and laughed. As we tiptoed around the beach towels and tanning girls, I could see Cyrus walking out of the water. He looked around the beach for a moment, and then recognizing us, he motioned his hand for us to come over. The cool breeze skimmed along my shoulders as I let the water glide over my toes. It wasn't cold enough to make you want to jump away and not warm enough to jump in for a swim either, just the perfect temperature that let you stand there satisfied.

"Did you girls see me?" Cyrus asked, running a hand through his wet tousled hair.

"Umm...well..." Kia began.

"Basically, you look like every other guy out there," Charlotte cut in. "So no, we didn't."

"But good job anyway!" Kia smiled.

"Thanks." Cyrus chuckled. "Maybe I should get you girls some binoculars."

"Or maybe you should just have a wetsuit the color of a traffic cone."

I pulled away from their conversation and looked out to the ocean. The sun was hitting it just perfectly; every time the water touched the shore, it made it look like a thousand shattering diamonds. It was too beautiful to ignore. So I flicked my camera on, looking through the lens. I was too close to get the shot I wanted, so I started to back up.

Suddenly, I felt something catch around my ankle; as I went to turn around to see what it was, it tugged just as I went to take a step back. I suddenly tripped and went falling forward, crashing to the ground.

I instantly felt something hard under me, and I knew it wasn't the sand. When I looked down, it was a boy.

"Oh my God."

"Actually, it's Maverick. Remember?"

There he was. Under me. So close. He was practically just a breath away. I could make out water droplets in his blonde hair. I hadn't realized how tan he was. His eyes were brighter today, too. Green? Not really. But not blue, either. Turquoise maybe? I felt dizzy.

He reached up and pressed his fingers lightly to my forehead. "Hit your head a little too hard?"

"No," I practically growled, pulling away from his touch.

"Feisty." He smirked. "You know, if you wanted to be on top of me you could've just asked." Then he did that thing boys do. That thing where he bit his lip and something flashed in his eyes, except this time he winked. My breath caught. Every horrible curse word was firing in my head as I pushed myself off him and started to storm away.

"Wait," he called, catching up with me. "Are you hurt?"

"No," I hissed.

He was suddenly in front of me, reaching out for my arm. "Are you sure?"

"Yes," I said, pulling away from him again. "Luckily, I had you to break my fall. And you're as hardheaded as they get."

I was surprised that he didn't look taken aback. The corner of his mouth lifted in a smile. "I know you don't hate me, Evelyn."

"You're right," I shot back, "I don't hate you. Because in order to hate you, I'd have to care about you. And by the way, it's Evie."

I didn't let him say another word. I spun right around, heading back towards Charlotte and Kia.

But not before I noticed the colors of his wetsuit, black and white, with just a hint of red.

NINE

"How many surf shops *are* there around here?" Charlotte asked, as we approached yet another one. It seemed like they outweighed clothing boutiques, grocery stores, schools; the list goes on and on.

"A lot. But this one is my favorite."

"That's what you said about the last ten."

"I mean it this time, though."

Cyrus pulled us into a surf shop with stickers covering the door, and a big sign outside that read "Galligans."

The building was tiny, and longer than it was wide with two rows of surfboards going straight down either side of the wall. And back farther were some clothes and wetsuits. A TV hung up in the far right corner, playing a surf movie.

My eyes found their way to a few surfboards. They were all different shapes and sizes but they all had similar artwork done on them. It was beautiful. Paintings in bright colors of waves and tiki masks, and big Hawaiian flowers.

"Hey there, lady."

I heard a voice below me, and I jumped away, startled. A kid who must have only been twelve with hair so blonde it could have been white was looking up at me with big gray eyes, his body sprawled out on the floor. His eyes went from the TV to me to the TV again.

"Sorry, I didn't see you there. I didn't step on you, did I?"

"Ow." He suddenly wailed, clutching his arm. "Oh, Lord have mercy, my arm!"

I looked at him, horrified. I couldn't have done that much damage; I hadn't even felt him under me.

"Are you okay?" I asked worriedly, kneeling so I could get a look at his arm.

"No, no. Don't touch it," he cried, and then all of a sudden his face became serious. "Unless you want to kiss me. I think that would make it feel better."

"Leave the poor girl alone, grom."

The boy burst into a fit of laughter, rolling down the floor.

"Sorry about that," a boy from behind the counter said with a laugh, his dreadlocks shaking with the motion. His skin was the color of a mocha, and even though he was built on the smaller side, he looked at least nineteen.

"I give him props for it."

He smiled shyly, and stuck out his hand. "Keegan."

"We call him Keego, though!" another little boy yelled.

"Evie."

I introduced Kia and Charlotte. And Cyrus explained our story to him. He had the craziest eyes I had ever seen, green with a red tint to them. They were almost hypnotizing.

"Keego does all the artwork on the boards."

"You did that?" I asked him, pointing to the set of boards I had been looking at earlier.

"It's nothing special."

"Are you kidding me?" Charlotte gawked, as she held one of the boards in her hands, working her fingers over the artwork. "This is brilliant."

Charlotte had always been a pretty good artist herself. I could almost see her fingers twitching for a pen. I could see the ideas starting to enter her head. She wanted to draw. Keego's work was inspiring. He caught the way the ocean makes you feel, through all its colors and forms.

Kia was just as infatuated. "What do you paint with?"

"One second; I'll show you." Keego ducked behind the counter for a moment, and quickly reappeared holding a few markers in his hands. "Paint pens."

"That's it?" Charlotte twirled a dark red one in her hand.

"Yup. That's it."

I could always appreciate good art, but I couldn't contribute. I could barely draw a stick figure. Clyde had always been the artistic one out of us two. He could just look at something, and suddenly it'd pour out of his fingertips on to a piece of paper. Just like that. As Charlotte, Kia, and Keego all talked about art, I took a seat on the floor with the groms. Cyrus had disappeared off to God knows where. He was probably out surfing, or hitting on girls. One of the two.

"What's your name?"

Suddenly, a big set of brown eyes was blinking up at me under long dark lashes.

"Evie," I told the little freckled face girl. "What's yours?"

She flashed a smile and she was missing at least three teeth. "Roxy."

Despite her dark eyes, she had a thick mess of curly blonde hair that was straight in some places and curly in the rest. She had a little lisp, so when she said her name it came out, "Rox-thee."

"And this is my twin brother, Robin." She pointed a finger into the chest of a boy sitting next to her. They looked identical.

The boy's, who had tried to get me to kiss him earlier, name was Sawyer. All three of them were rambunctious. They shot a million questions at me a minute. Questions of sharks, and boyfriends, and everything else under the sun. All trying to get my attention. But I couldn't help but notice the fourth member of their group. He was sitting in the corner by one of the boards, staring at us the whole time. He had bright green eyes and dark hair that came just past his ears.

"Who's your friend over there?"

"That's Oliver," Roxy answered, quickly.

"Why is he all the way over there?"

"He doesn't like to talk to people. My mom says he's like austixic," Robin said.

"You mean autistic?"

"Yeah, something like that."

For some reason, the boy reminded me of myself. I remember during all my mom's fancy parties, and my dad's business meetings, I was always the kid in the corner, with a book in my hand or my headphones in. It's not that I didn't want to interact with everyone. I just didn't know how to. Do you ever feel like you're always on a different page than everyone else? Do you ever feel like sometimes you're in a whole different book than everyone else? That's how I felt. Disconnected.

I was going to try to talk to Oliver. Maybe not today. Maybe he needed time to warm up to me. But someday I'd talk to him. I'd help him get the confidence to join his friends and be a kid.

Cyrus finally stumbled back into Galligans with a big Hawaiian guy towering over behind him.

"I almost got that chick's number, dude."

"Sure, son." The Hawaiian roared with laughter. "We all know you do well with the *wahines*."

The minute the Hawaiian guy spotted the girls and me, he ran a hand through his black mane of hair, and flashed a smile.

"Hey ladies, I'm Kekoa. Where you girls from?"

The kids had suddenly gone quiet as soon as he had entered the surf shop.

"You won't know where it is," Charlotte warned him.

He stared at her unblinkingly. "Try me."

"Mokelumne Hill," Kia answered.

"Where the hell is that?"

Charlotte and Kia both started giggling. "Middle of nowhere."

"Mokelumne Hill is located in Calaveres County. Home of the Miwok Indians."

Kia's mouth dropped open. "How did you?"

"He knows everything," Cyrus interrupted.

Kekoa suddenly turned serious, his stare intense. "You want to know why I know everything? Because of how I was raised. I grew up in a military family. On my island."

He was pacing the room now, running his hands over the surfboards. His voice got louder with every word as he spoke. "Kids nowadays aren't raised correctly. They're disrespectful, arrogant, barnacles." After he finished his rant, he was calm again. But there was a sternness that didn't leave his face. And then a light hit his eyes.

"So are you girls ready to surf?"

TEN

The next week passed by as quickly as a wave. Charlotte,
Kia, and I didn't even get dressed in clothes half the time. We
woke up and threw on our bikinis. We lounged on the beach as
Cyrus surfed, and spent the rest of the day doing whatever we felt
like. We were eager to learn to surf, too, and Kekoa promised to
take us out after the Fourth of July. He was slammed with surf
lessons until then. Some days, we'd go to the markets, sampling
every piece of sweet fruit and letting it melt in our mouths as we
savored it. Other days, we sat on the side of the sidewalk, simply
people watching. No matter what we did, I took my camera
everywhere. I was constantly feeling as if I needed to capture the
moment. I was so used to sitting in Soleil, watching the rain
dribble down the windows. And now here I was, practically a
storm raging around me. So much was going on, all the time. I
didn't want to miss a thing.

We went to Galligans almost every single day, and we were
all starting to get to know the kids there pretty well. We would sit
and watch Keego paint his boards. And we eventually even
started helping out behind the counter with a charming twenty-
year-old guy named Vince. Young surfers constantly poured
throughout the shop, coming to just hangout and help sell boards
or watch surf videos on the TV screen. Keegan and Vince called
them the "groms," which basically meant they were the young

surfers. The "babies" were there, too: Sawyer, Roxy, Robin, and Oliver.

Even though we hadn't been in Waverly for that long, we were already starting to get used to the pace of things. Tina had taken us to her clothing store downtown, a cute, beachy girls' clothing boutique that was wedged right between a gelato place and a vintage store. A pink surfboard and dream catchers hung in the window; a bright yellow sign hung over the door that read, "Luna's."

Tina pulled us through the crowd of girls that were gathered inside, drooling over the string bikinis. "Take whatever you want," she told us.

We argued with her for a while, but finally, after her convincing us that she was way too stocked up with clothes and we were actually doing her a favor, we started shopping. I had never really liked shopping. I just didn't find clothes that interesting; to be perfectly honest, they were kind of annoying. I'd much rather just be in a bathing suit all day. With that being said, I headed straight for the bathing suit section, which took up most of the store. There were so many: floral ones, sparkly ones, studded ones, stringy ones.

"Ah, ah, ah," I heard Charlotte say as I reached for the most covering blue one I could find.

Oh gosh, I thought as I watched her scanning the walls. Charlotte was a lot more racy than I was. For instance, at my 8[th]grade slumber party, I wore a cute pair of pajama pants. Charlotte showed up in a frilly nightgown from Victoria's Secret, looking as if she had just come back from a photo shoot.

"Perfect," she said, as she reached up and snatched a white string bikini off the wall and handed it to me. "You're hot. You're young. Flaunt it or get inside." She winked, and walked slowly towards the dressing room.

After I shimmied into it, I did a little turn in the mirror. The bikini was little. Not too tight little. Just not a lot of fabric little. The white *did* make me look super tan. I was shocked by the amount of cleavage I suddenly had. My mom was tall and flat as a pancake. I had gotten my height from her, but I wondered where I had gotten my boobs from. I studied myself in the mirror. I guess I did have a somewhat good body. But there was no way I could wear this in front of people. I was conservative. Heck, I had lawyers as parents. Even my mom went to work in a suit.

"I'm not going outside in this," I yelled at Charlotte over the dressing room door.

"Let me see!" I could hear Kia's voice coming from the dressing room next to me.

"How about not."

"Evie. If you don't come out here then I'm going in," Charlotte threatened.

"Fine," I moaned. I pulled the door open just a crack. "See?"

Charlotte yanked the door open all the way, and I immediately backed up farther into the dressing room, hoping no one could see me.

"Damn," was all she said.

I raised my eyebrow. "Damn?"

"Wow," Kia suddenly said, appearing in the doorway, wearing a cute, sparkly purple suit.

Charlotte, Kia, and I skinny dipped in the lake every summer. I never felt awkward in front of them. But I felt as if I was standing there asking them how I looked in sexy lingerie.

"You're buying it," Charlotte demanded, right before I shut the door on them.

We ended up leaving Tina's store with three bags of clothes per girl. Shorts, flip flops, cut-off shirts, and bathing suits practically overflowed every bag. Needless to say, the white bikini had come with me.

The next day when we were about to go to the beach, I wasn't allowed to leave until I put it on. Cyrus just stared at me when I walked out of the house, which made me feel ten times more uncomfortable than I had before. The whistles on the beach didn't help, either. I'm pretty sure by the time we left, I was as red as a tomato and about ready to drown Charlotte. By the end of the week, I had gotten used to it.

I hadn't seen Maverick and I was glad. I didn't need another run-in with him. Sometimes as I was walking down Main, I wondered where he was, though, and what he was doing. Then I'd wonder at why I wondered about him. Words were always twisting around in my head, things I wanted to say to him. I couldn't believe Maverick was the same guy that had been on that beautiful wave. He didn't seem like the same person.

By the end of the day, we were all exhausted. And no matter how much sunscreen we slathered on, we always seemed to climb into bed with somewhat burned skin, crazy wind-churned hair, and heavy lids.

ELEVEN

The Fourth of July.

It had never been a big holiday in Mokelumne Hill. People hung flags and that was about it. Fireworks were illegal. And the town was so small, if you even tried anything, the cops would hunt you down within the hour.

But the whole week that's all everyone ever talked about. "So what are you doing for the Fourth?" I got asked at least twenty times.

I finally asked Cyrus what the big hype was about. He explained that in Waverly they practically honored the Fourth of July. It wasn't just like any other holiday. It was *the* holiday. They started the morning off with a huge parade. And because fireworks weren't illegal in Waverly, the whole rest of the night was history.

We woke up fairly early to get to the parade. Tina had ridden her bike down to Main and it was completely decked out with streamers, flags, and bows. In fact, a whole heard of people had their bikes decorated. They rode down to Main Street in one big movement, completely taking over the streets. There was so much excitement in the air, you could practically smell it. A sea of red, white, and blue people. I was waiting for them to all bust out in dance like a musical or something.

As I got closer to Main Street, I realized just how crazy it really was. Crowds were in front of every store, people racing across the street in a hurry trying to find a spot to sit and watch the parade. Because Tina owned Luna's Boutique, she luckily already had a spot waiting for her. We sat on the sidewalk in front of her store and watched the chaos before the parade started. I lifted my camera up and snapped a photo.

I wondered whether a year from now I'd be able to look at this picture and remember this exact feeling. The feeling of anticipation and electricity buzzing through your whole body. The high you get off a crowd of hopeful people.

The parade finally started and the floats that began to pass by were incredible. The school cheerleaders and dancers fluttered through the streets, following their pattern. But most of the floats were representing all the local's shops. We all cheered as Galligans passed by us. The owner of the small surf shop was up at the front of it, waving to everyone below. Cyrus suddenly latched on to the side of the float and climbed up on top of it, joining Keego and Vince. They both laughed and helped pull him up.

The next float was Swells'. Theirs was covered in pretty girls dancing in hula skirts and a guy playing a ukulele. On each side were a few surfers, holding up their boards with a smile. Of course, Maverick was on my side. He had a smoldering expression on his face, and he looked unamused. I barely missed him. And from the corner of my eye, I swear I saw him wink at me.

That night, Tina had gone out to the bars and told us to all stay inside. I was lying in bed, listening to the fireworks and the sound of police cars, when I heard footsteps enter our room, a loud banging sound, like something knocking over, a curse word, and then silence.

"Girls, are you awake?"

Silence again.

"I am," I answered. "What's up?"

Kia had woken up, and she walked to the side of the room to the light switch.

"What the hell?" Charlotte moaned, groggily, as soon as the light had flicked on. "Is there a fire?"

"No."

"Then why did you wake me up?"

"Noah just called me. There's this huge bonfire party down at the beach. We gotta go."

She blinked at him a few times. "What time is it?"

"It's only eleven, Charlotte."

She seemed more awake now that he had mentioned a party. "Well, I can't sleep now."

He grinned widely. "I'm going. If you girls care to join, meet me at the van in ten, and be quiet."

After we all stumbled into our clothes, and tried to look somewhat hot, we snuck downstairs as quietly as we could. Kia and Charlotte rubbed at their eyes, but I was wide awake and excited. I had been waiting for something like this.

Cyrus was already waiting for us out at the van. When we climbed in, there were cases of beer taking up most of our seats. We just sat on the floor, huddling together so there was room.

When we pulled up to the parking lot in front of the beach, there were tons of cars everywhere. As we jumped out of the car, I could see the bonfire burning bright ahead, a crowd of people surrounding it.

"Now girls, there's a couple of rules," Cyrus said to us as he unloaded the cases of beers. "I told Clyde I'd take care of you guys.

"Rule one." He pointed his finger to the back of a truck where a boy and girl where screwing around. "If I find any of you doing that, I'll kill the guy. Keep your clothes on.

"Rule two. Don't get drunk off your ass. I don't have enough arms to take care of you all. Also, stick together.

"And rule three," he said, with a wink. "Have fun."

Suddenly, Cyrus had disappeared into the cluster of people, blending in with every other shirtless tan boy. I wondered whether by the end of the night we'd even be able to find him. I had only been to one party before. It was a house party, and Charlotte had dragged me along. By the time we got there, there were people everywhere: on the stairs, in the bathroom, in the bedrooms. I remember feeling so suffocated by the walls of the house, and the loudness of the people and the smell of beer and the stupid techno music and bright lights. I just wanted out. I waited outside on the porch until Charlotte stumbled out of the front door, unbelievably drunk. I helped her to the car and drove her home and that was that.

But this was different. Music blasted from one of the cars in the parking lot; everyone was huddled together, laughing and drinking; the only source of light came from the bright fire and full moon.

"Hey guys!" Noah smiled, pushing through the crowd.

We all said hey. I looked over at Kia and she was already blushing. Charlotte pushed her closer to him, and he reached out and gave her a hug. She turned as red as the fire.

Charlotte gestured towards his empty hands. "Where's your beer?"

"I don't drink," he said, easily. As if he were merely saying, *I don't like Sprite.*

"Really?" Charlotte asked, surprised.

"Really," he answered. He raised an eyebrow at Kia. "Are you cold?"

"Oh, no...I'm fine." Kia was clearly shivering, though.

He took her hand gently. "C'mon, I'll take you over to the fire."

I gave Kia a look. You know—the *Are you good with it* look —and she nodded with a smile.

"Nice boy," Charlotte admitted, as they disappeared back

into the cluster of people. "Now, let's go find some drinks."

It didn't take any time at all.

"Would you like a beer?"

We were only halfway through the crowd, when the tall bronzed boy offered us the two iced cold beers in his hands. He had an Australian accent, and it came out more like, *Would you like a bee-yur?*

"Thanks." Charlotte smiled at him seductively, taking both of them and pushing one of them into my hand without even looking at me. "Australia, yeah?"

"How'd ya know?" He raised his arm and rested his hand on the back of his neck, clearly flexing.

"I'm good with accents." Charlotte flirted. She pursed her lips, obviously making them look more kissable, and then took a slow sip of the beer.

After a few minutes, I was tired of hearing Charlotte flirt. I made sure she had her phone, and faded back into the group of people once more. I decided I should probably check on Kia, and I made my way towards the bonfire. The beer was ice cold in my hand. It felt a little strange, like it should've been a Coke or a bottle of water, but it wasn't. I pressed the bottle to my lips and took a big gulp. The coldness of it felt good against my throat, even though the aftertaste was kind of gross. I made a face, and took another one, and then another one. I couldn't tell whether I liked it or I hated it.

A girl suddenly bumped into me. Her eyes fluttered when she talked. "Isn't it just so nice out?" she droned.

"Sure," I said. And it *was* nice out. The air was still warm but the breeze was cool and it intensified the smell of beer and cologne and salt. And now with her standing there in front of me, the smell of weed was mixed in, too.

She held a joint up between her fingers, offering it to me with a lazy half smile. I hesitated, staring at it for a moment. I had never tried smoking before. To be honest, it always seemed pretty disgusting to me. But so did beer, and here I was chugging it down.

"Maybe in a little," I told her. I was still undecided. I moved past her, not having the patience to wait for her slow reply, and kept walking towards the fire.

Even though there were at least twenty people sitting around the fire, I spotted Kia and Noah easily. They were the only ones without a drink, and they both had clothes on. Noah was resting his head on her shoulder, and he was running his hand down her long dark hair. They looked as if they were talking. I didn't want to interrupt them, so I craned around to see whether I could find Charlotte again.

All of a sudden, my heart stopped as I noticed a guy straight in front of me. I felt as if I couldn't breathe. It couldn't be. There was no way. But it looked *exactly* like him. I closed in the few feet between us, and reached out my hand to touch his arm. I just needed to see his eyes, and then I'd know it was him. "Clyde."

"Nope," the guy said, turning around to face me. "My name's Dusty."

I noticed his eyes were green, and he really didn't look like Clyde at all.

He was standing next to another guy with hair the color of raven. "I'm Wes."

I ignored both of them, and turned back around, my heart clattering around in my chest.

The disappointment was almost too much to bear. I suddenly felt tears in my eyes. I pressed the beer back against my lips, finishing off the whole bottle. I urgently felt the need to find the girl with the joint again. I pressed back into the crowd, trying to remember what she looked like. She had to be somewhere close by. I had just seen her. I grabbed another beer from someone along the way. I spent a good fifteen minutes trying to find her. I eventually gave up on it. Feeling frustrated, I fell away from the flock of people, moving closer to the water. By that point, I was already feeling buzzed.

Everything felt slower. My legs felt heavier as I walked. But my mind felt lighter, too. It numbed the pain; it numbed everything. I was far away from the the party now. I could barely make out the fire when I looked back. And everything was dark, except for the moon glowing along the water.

"Hey cutie."

The voice sent a shock down my spine. I had figured I was alone, but when I turned around, there was a guy following me.

He wasn't very tall, and he wasn't built like a surfer either. He was stocky; he looked strong.

I turned back around and kept walking. I wasn't interested in a boy taking my mind off things. The beer was already doing a pretty good job of that.

"Hey, I'm talking to you." His voice was louder now, angry almost. And I could hear a slur in them.

I didn't turn around this time, or stop, either. But I could feel him getting closer to me. My instincts went into overdrive, but the buzz was still making me feel too slow to react fast enough.

Just keep walking. Just keep walking.

Suddenly I felt his grubby hand grab at my arm; his breathing was loud and ragged and I felt as if his chubby body could collapse on to me any second.

"Let me go," I demanded loudly, trying to yank away from him.

I went to reach for my phone, knowing it was too late. His hand stayed locked on my arm. I tried again to pull away but he didn't budge an inch.

"Don't fight, cutie. It's no use."

I didn't know what else to do. My throat felt dry and I couldn't talk, so I screamed. He lurched forward to cover my mouth, and I turned around and suddenly I threw my fist towards his face. He let go of me for a second, and clutched at his nose.

"You're going to pay for that."

I tried to run up the sand but it felt as if I wasn't going anywhere. He reached out to grab me again, but I leapt forward, crashing into the sand, just missing his grasp. My head collided hard onto one of the large rocks on the beach. His voice faded as I lost consciousness.

~~

I felt someone touch me again and I flinched until I realized it was softer now. "Hey, you're fine."

It was another boy. And this one was lifting me up, carrying me to God knows where. I didn't really care. My fist hurt from punching the guy and I was too freaked out. Too weak. Way too dizzy. My head was aching.

I heard the guy yelling again, the one who had tried to attack me. "Calm down, dude...she wanted it."

He sounded as though he was talking to someone. There was another voice; I didn't know who it belonged to, but whoever it was sounded very angry.

Their conversation faded as the guy carried me farther away. I noticed we were in the parking lot, but there were only two cars. He opened the door to a black truck, and set me in the passenger seat gently. He looked me over, and sighed. In the moonlight, I could just make out his build. He was small. And as he dipped farther into the car, I could see the outline of freckles on his face. His hair had droplets of water in it and looked dark auburn, almost red, but maybe that was just the lighting.

My throat was still so dry, and now felt burned from screaming. I struggled to get words out, and when I did they were barely audible. "Who are you?"

"I'm Peter."

He opened a bottle of water for me and pushed it into my hand. "I think you should drink. It'll make you feel better."

I nodded once and took a small sip. It hurt my throat at first, but after a couple more sips I felt as if I could talk again.

"He-he tried to—"

"Don't worry," Peter said calmly. "I know what happened. It's okay. It's all taken care of."

His eyes stayed patient with me. He reached up and moved a piece of hair off my face, his eyes kind of sad.

"Thanks."

"Don't thank me." I heard someone climb into the front seat. "Thank him."

I looked up and there he was. I was suddenly thrown into a world of blue, just like every time I saw him.

"Hi," Maverick murmured. His eyes were so bright, they lit up the whole car.

"How is she?" he asked, looking to Peter.

"Better, I think."

"I can talk." I blurted, "I'm fine."

Maverick and Peter both looked at me and then back at each other. "I'll take her home. I know where Cyrus lives. Thanks, bud."

Peter nodded towards me. "Feel better."

He knocked fists with Maverick. "Later," he said, closing the door.

The noise made my head hurt. I sat up in the passenger seat and I ached. I looked at Maverick. "What are you doing here?"

"This is my truck." He turned around, looking behind him as he put the truck into reverse and backed out of the parking space. The truck launched forward as he changed gears. I just sat there and stared at him.

He was wearing board shorts and a black shirt with a crown on it, which I found oddly fitting and kind of funny, because he had come to my rescue. He looked over at me and I quickly looked away.

"Out of everyone who could've found me." I stared out the window; everything felt faded. "Of course, it had to be you."

He was staring straight ahead, a smirk playing on his lips. "I guess you were just lucky."

"I didn't need to be saved, you know. You showed up right after I punched him."

"You punched him?" he asked, gawking at me.

I nodded. "How'd you find me, anyway?"

"Peter and I had just finished surfing, and we heard you scream."

That explained why Peter's hair was wet.

"Surfing?" I argued; it was stupid because it didn't matter, anyway. "But it's dark out."

"Full moon. And the fireworks help some."

"Why weren't you out getting drunk?"

"I have a contest tomorrow. Besides, Nationals are at the end of the month. "

"Oh. I just thought you'd be at the party," I admitted.

"Is that why you went?" he asked playfully, his eyes holding me for a second.

I was glad that it was dark in the car, because I felt heat in my cheeks as I looked away. Just then a firework shot off. I could just make it out in the rearview mirror. It was the kind that looked like dripping gold rain. Those had always been my favorite.

"I don't like you, remember?"

"Mhhmmm," he hummed. "Keep telling yourself that, babe."

I felt heat spread all over me now, practically making me feel as if I was on fire. I snuck a glance up at him, and he was still staring straight ahead. As I sat there, I realized I had never looked at him long enough to really take in his features. He had long, light eyelashes, bright eyes. A kind of long boyish nose that tied into full lips. He was too pretty. Too pretty to even be real, it seemed like.

My eyes fell to his hands and suddenly something on them gleamed as the light from a stoplight hit them. It took me a second to realize it was blood.

"Your hands." I took one of them off the steering wheel and turned it in my own. "You're bleeding."

"It's not mine." His voice was low as he pulled his hand away.

Then I remembered the sound of him arguing with the guy as I had been picked up off the ground.

"You hit him," I accused, breathlessly.

"He needed to be taught. That can't happen to you again."

His voice was much different now, angry. He clenched his jaw, and became quiet.

I wanted to take his hand again, feel the jolt when he touched me, but I was afraid he might pull away.

The truck suddenly stopped and I realized with a start we were already at the house. I didn't know what to say. I felt overwhelmed. I had pretty much despised Maverick. How was it that he was the one who had helped me tonight? And now he was sitting here, practically an angel. A tormented one.

I watched him run a hand through his blonde hair, and push his head back against his seat, closing his eyes. "Please, be more careful. I swear, I could have killed him."

I felt dizzy again, but I was sure it wasn't from the alcohol anymore. I wanted to reach out and touch him, but I was afraid he'd disappear underneath the tips of my fingers. So I forced myself to look away.

"Goodnight, Evie," he murmured, as I reached for the door. "Sweet dreams."

TWELVE

I'll never forget the night Clyde came home with a swollen lip, blood dripping down his chin and leaking onto his shirt.

"What happened to you?" I asked him as soon as he walked in the door.

Most guys liked to brag about fighting; the minute after it happens they'll tell anyone who will listen. Always twisting the story to make it sound as if they were the tough one. But Clyde wasn't like that. He wasn't proud of hurting people, so all he told me was, "Go to sleep."

"No, you gotta tell me," I said. "Or else I'll just hear it from someone else."

Moke Hill was way too small of a town. If you fought someone, you better be prepared to hear about it everywhere. It might as well have been televised and called a boxing match.

"I was at the gas station. And this guy was just being an ass to this girl."

"Did you know them?"

"No."

"You didn't even know the girl?" I pressed.

"Nope."

I studied his swollen lip, and winced. "So why get involved?"

Clyde started dabbing at his lip with a wet washcloth, not even flinching. "Because it was wrong. And I was there. I saw it. I couldn't just let it happen."

"He hit her," I assumed. "Wow."

He didn't answer, just kept dabbing at his cut.

"How does he look?"

Clyde somehow cracked a smile. "Worse than me."

That was who Clyde was. Someone who did things for others. People that he didn't even know, people that could never repay him. He wasn't cocky; he didn't assume people liked him. He was just a good person. I had never considered Maverick one of those people. Until now.

I took a deep breath and ran my hand through my hair, pulling my side bangs over the small cut I had gotten from the rock, and opened the door.

"Holy shit, Evie." Charlotte ran to me as soon as I entered the house. "Where the hell have you been?"

"I went on a walk."

I was too exhausted to tell the story. My head was still fuzzy. My fist still hurt. I just wanted to go to sleep and forget this whole night.

"A walk?" Cyrus appeared in the doorway, his face strained. "Do you know how worried we were about you?"

Kia threw her arms around me, sniffling. She sounded as if she had been crying.

"I'm sorry." I tried to sound convincing. "I got lost."

I guess the second part was somewhat true.

Cyrus's voice was suddenly loud. "I told you guys to stay together."

"Relax," I told Cyrus. "I'm home now. I'm a big girl, you know. I can take care of myself."

"Your brother left me in charge of you. Do you know how horrible I'd feel if anything happened? He trusted me."

"Who cares?" My voice was shaking. "He's dead."

Cyrus's mouth dropped, his face stunned. I was sure Charlotte and Kia's expression was the same. I didn't care. I was only looking at Cyrus.

"He's missing, Evie."

"Missing?" I yelled. "My parents buried him a long time ago. All they were missing was a body."

"He could still be out there."

"He's not!" I hissed. "Go find yourself a new best friend because he's never coming back."

And there it was. The expression of brokenness etching its

way across Cyrus's face. I had seen it so many times before—on my father, my mother, even myself. But I had caused it this time.

I knew the pain of losing someone. It's a feeling you can't describe. It's not just internal; it's physical. Your body aches. There's this weight in your chest, and it feels like you can't even breathe. The pain is bad, but then there's the numbness. There's the part of losing someone where you feel nothing at all. And I believe that is the worst thing death does to us. It detaches us. It holds us down.

"Shit." I cursed as tears started streaming down my cheeks. I couldn't stop them. But I wanted desperately to. I was losing it and I was falling, crumpling to the ground as if I were five again. My whole body shook with sobs. I didn't feel like me. I felt as if I was outside of me, watching myself falling apart. The alcohol had faded and the pain was back. The feeling of hoping, praying, that it was Clyde in front of me. The disappointment when I realized it wasn't and that it never would be. It didn't matter if I was downtown or at the surf shop or at the beach. Clyde wouldn't be there.

And I realized I had never truly let it hit me. I just pretended that he had gotten in his car and drove away to Waverly, that he was only pretending to be dead, that maybe, just maybe he was one of the few lucky people that survived the plane crash.

I was in another set of arms. This time, it was Cyrus. He swooped me up and he didn't say anything. I felt the rhythm of us moving up flights of stairs; I was sure I was falling asleep.

I felt my head hit the pillow softly, and the warmness of my comforter as it was tucked around me. And I wanted to say thank you, or say anything for that matter. But I was already falling into a dream.

I was at the beach, but everything was fuzzy again. The colors of the sky and the ocean blurred together. The sand was hot, hot on my feet. It made them sting, but it felt good. Then I was being handed that little object again—long, pointy. It had to be a key.

Except this time, it wasn't Clyde giving it to me. It was Maverick.

THIRTEEN

I was still thinking about the key that had appeared in two of my dreams. Clyde had never mentioned anything about it. And I couldn't imagine what it could possibly be to. I figured it was probably my mind just making things up, because it didn't make any sense. I let it occupy my thoughts while I lay sprawled out on the carpet in Galligans. Keego was sitting next to me, a board balancing on his legs. He was already starting to outline waves on it with one of his paint pens.

"Hey Keego, could you check the back for me and see if we have any smalls in the Bolsa and Sugar Bomb shirts?" Vince called from behind the counter. He was at the register, flirting with a tall brunette who was standing on the other side.

Keego was too infatuated with his painting so I decided to go look for him. The back room was full of stuff: clothes, shoes, broken boards, old wetsuits. I quickly looked through the rack of shirts, and found what I was looking for. Just as I was about to head back, a logo caught my eye. It was the same one that had been on Clyde's hat that was in his room. The one that I had found the key under.

At first, I figured the board wasn't anything special. Tons of people had that sticker on their board. But as I looked closer, I realized there was a design on the bottom of it. I set the shirts down, and flipped the board over carefully. The image on the back was one I had seen a million times: it was the same drawing Clyde had hung up on his wall in his room. He had drawn it the first time he had come back from Waverly. My hands felt weak, and I felt as if I could drop the board at any second so I put it back carefully. Had this been Clyde's board? It was wonderful finding it, as if I were beginning to find pieces of a missing puzzle. But it was also overwhelming, because I kept wanting to forget the puzzle had broken apart. I picked up the shirts and walked back into the shop, handing them to Vince.

"You good?" Vince asked me as soon as the brunette had left. "You look like you just saw a ghost or something."

"I'm fine."

Keego suddenly looked up from his painting, setting his paint pen down. "What's up? Talk to us, grom."

"I just found a board in the back room. That's all."

Vince and Keego both raised their eyebrows, waiting for me to give them more information. There was no way to really steer around the subject.

"It just had one of Clyde's drawings on it," I said easily.

"Oh," Vince said slowly.

Keego's eyes darted back to his board. They both didn't speak for a few minutes. I immediately felt like an idiot for even bringing it up. I was so good at being way too honest and then making things awkward.

Keego's voice was almost too quiet to make out. "It's his, Evie."

My heart gave a hard thump in my chest, almost painful. "Oh."

"We were going to give it to you," Keego murmured. "But we couldn't decide between you and..."

"And who?"

Keego had started drawing aimlessly on his hand, clearly anxious. "And Clyde's girlfriend."

"Girlfriend?" I asked, stunned.

Vince had made his way back behind the counter, and he was now counting change.

"Vince?"

"Vince isn't here," he announced.

Clyde had never once mentioned anything about a girlfriend, or a girl at all for that matter. He was too busy raving about surfboards and the ocean and his "mates."

"Well, I have the right to at least know who she is," I demanded.

Keego suddenly grabbed my hand gently. I felt the wet paint pen soak into my skin for a quick second and when he pulled away, there was an address and a name scrawled on it. "Go see for yourself."

As Vince and Keego had gone completely mute, I lingered outside the surf shop for a while, wondering whether it was a good idea to go to her house. I mean, wasn't that kind of weird? Just having your dead boyfriend's sister suddenly ringing your doorbell? And what was the point, anyway?

But my mind kept going back to the key, and maybe, just maybe she had some kind of information. As I watched people walk down Main Street, I studied the girls that passed me. And it only made me wonder more what Clyde's girlfriend looked like, what her personality was like. I realized I didn't care whether it was a bad idea or not. I was doing it anyway. I couldn't help but feel slightly angry at the fact that she might get his board over me. I was his sister. His best friend.

My hands were sweaty as I suddenly arrived in front of a small white house. It was cute, the kind you see in magazines with the perfect picket fence to match. I glanced at my hand again to make sure I had the address right. I forced myself to knock on the door. The knock was light with my nervousness—too light, I worried she wouldn't hear it. I prayed that she didn't.

My heart fell to my stomach as the door swung open slowly, and then it did a flip as I realized who it was smiling back at me.

"Oh, hello."

It was the same girl who worked at Kae's Point. The one who had smiled at me and Kia while we were in line. Who I always found peeking at me as I walked by. She had always been so friendly, and I never understood why.

"Hi." I managed to get out.

She kept the same shy smile on her face, using the same tone she had probably used in the cafe all the time. "Can I help you with something?"

"I'm looking for Maddi."

She smiled crookedly. "Here."

I couldn't put words together. There was nothing I could say that would make me not look crazy. I was doomed no matter what way you sliced it.

"Okay, this is going to sound kind of weird but I...well, I'm Clyde's sister. And I guess you guys had a thing. And I thought I might as well, like, come and actually meet you."

Even I realized how strange I sounded, so I decided just to shut up.

Her voice was like honey. "Of course I know you're his sister. He always talked about you."

Again, I had that feeling as if I couldn't breathe. That tugging at my heart.

I sighed with relief and held out my hand. "Evie."

She suddenly threw her arms around me in a hug. "I'm Maddi. It's so nice to finally meet you."

As she pulled away, she studied me, and her eyes turned sad. She didn't try to hide it; she was like an open book.

"You have his eyes. And his freckles. You look just like him."

"I get that a lot," I admitted.

"I suppose you came here for a reason, though."

I was already starting to look for an excuse as to why I was there, when all of a sudden the glow from the sun caught something shiny hanging around her neck. It glittered as the light hit it, like a little diamond. But longer, sharper. A key.

"What does that key open?" I asked her, gesturing towards it.

She caught it in her fingers and squeezed it.

"Nothing now." Her voice was sad. "It was the key to Clyde and I's apartment. We were just about to move in...but then...after the crash, I didn't wanna live by myself so I decided to come back home. I still kept the key, though. I guess I'm still hoping one day he'll come back."

It was so simple. It was just a little key. That's all. But it held so much value. It held a future. A promise. And now all of it was gone. I wasn't the only one hoping he would come home.

FOURTEEN

"Are you girls ready?"

The ocean looked tranquil today. At least, at the moment it did. It was always changing. In a half an hour, it could be different. In ten minutes, it could be different. You just never really know when it comes to the ocean. I had been waiting to go surfing. Kekoa had met us out at the beach; the same serious expression was still on his face from last time I had seen him. He was intimidating. But comforting, too. I knew as long as we were out there with him, we'd be fine.

"What if I see a shark?" Charlotte asked him, as she zipped up her wetsuit.

It was ridiculous how she still looked like a model.

"Then you see a shark."

Charlotte shot him a look. "Could I touch it?"

"Sure. Touch it with whatever arm you want to lose." Cyrus chuckled.

"Pick up your board. C'mon. Hustle," Kekoa told her.

Noah had Kia's board tucked under his arm. And Cyrus was standing next to me.

I had never been scared of the water, and I guess that's probably what resulted in me drowning at eleven years old. It wasn't even that I was a bad swimmer. I was actually a pretty strong one. But it was my first time going to a beach, and I had been so overwhelmed by the beauty of the ocean, I just completely lost myself in it. My parents expected me to never go in the water again. But I was right back in there the next day. Clyde had stayed with me, making sure I didn't go too far again.

As I rested my hand on the surfboard and pushed it over the small whitewash, walking out farther into the water, I realized fear was the last thing I felt in the ocean. If anything, I felt more scared on land. Out in the water, you don't have to pretend. It's you and the ocean. And that's all.

All of a sudden, I realized someone else's hand was on the board. It wasn't Cyrus's. Tan, long fingers. I already knew who it was. I looked up and he was smirking at me.

"Are you stalking me?"

He was wearing the same wetsuit, black and white with a little bit of red. He walked through the water calmly, as if he were simply strolling down the sidewalk. As much as I hated to admit it, my heart was racing at the fact that he was there.

"I'll leave you two." Cyrus smiled, heading towards Charlotte and Kekoa.

"Not quite." He came around the board so he was standing next to me, and now only he was in control of it. "I just like to help a damsel in distress when I see one."

"Well then, maybe you should go help Kia."

He traced his fingers lightly over my hand, leaving the skin where he touched tingling. "I'd rather help you."

"I thought you had a contest."

"I have a little time between heats."

We were waist high in the water now, and past the whitewash stage. I could see the waves started to form farther out. I could feel the anxiousness building in my stomach.

"Up," he said, tapping the deck.

"This is the only time I will ever listen to you," I warned him, as I climbed up onto the board.

It was sturdy under me; it felt right, but I could still feel the nervousness in my stomach.

He took my hands gently in his and rested them in the water. "Try paddling."

I thought for a minute and tried to remember exactly how I had seen surfers do it. They dipped their hands into the water, cupping it, pulling it back, and doing it all over again.

I started to paddle and the board began to glide along the water. He stopped for a second, and touched my back. "Good. Just get a rhythm; pull the water. Think of running."

Running, I thought. What did running and surfing have to do with each other?

But he was the expert, so as I started to paddle again, I thought of running. I thought of the rhythm you picked up when you jogged. *One. Two. One. Two.*

Maverick suddenly grabbed the board and flipped it around slowly so I was facing the beach. He held me in place as he looked over his shoulder. I felt a little dizzy.

His voice was calm, steady. "This one's you."

"Umm."

"Paddle."

My arms felt as if they weren't going to work for a minute, and then I imagined the surfers again in my head. I could hear the water building behind me as I started to paddle. *One. Two. One. Two. One.*

"Up."

Just as I pushed off the board and landed on my feet, I could feel the board drop into the wave. My heart stopped and I quickly pushed my weight back to guide my board back to the top of the wave. It was like a game, almost. Playing with the ocean. Except, she was temperamental and powerful, and she'd always win if she wanted to. I felt like today she was being easy on me. The wave crumbled and I jumped off my board, catching it with my hands just in time as another set started to roll in.

I couldn't stop smiling as I paddled back towards Maverick. After a moment, I realized he was smiling, too. I felt the nervous ache make itself apparent in my stomach again.

"What is it?" I asked him as soon as I was close enough.

"I just can't believe you don't live by the ocean."

The water was just brimming against his crossed arms, and his eyes reflected the green coming off my board. I couldn't get over the feeling of always wanting him closer.

"What's that supposed to mean?"

He hesitated, his fingers skimming along the rails of my board. "You just belong here."

Then he suddenly sunk deeper into the water, completely disappearing.

"Maverick?" I called, looking around.

I felt something hit my board, hard. I steadied myself back on it, starting to feel the fidgety ball in my stomach roll around. Then, abruptly, my board flipped over.

Shark.

I detangled myself from it and swam quickly to the top, latching on to my board in fear, only to see Maverick floating there, laughing.

"Gotcha," he said, grabbing my hand.

I pulled away from him, splashing water towards his face. "You're a jerk."

But I couldn't even be mad. Something about his laugh was too much like a child's. Light and innocent. And obviously contagious, because I started laughing, too. I guess we were just kids, after all.

"I have to go now," Maverick murmured, checking his watch. He was so close to me. Close enough to see the water droplets on his eyelids, his lips. "Come watch the contest later."

I struggled to form a witty response. "Maybe. If I have nothing better to do."

He laughed, and then leaned in even closer. My heart stopped, and I thought for a second he might try to kiss me. But instead, he reached forward and moved my wet hair away from my face, his lips resting by my ear.

"I promise. I'm better than whatever else you have planned."

FIFTEEN

I came in from the ocean a few hours later, the taste of salt heavy in my mouth. Wet, tangled hair. Burning eyes. Water still brimming in my throat. My arms feeling like noodles. And I loved it. I loved every single drop of it.

My arms ached as I helped load the boards back into the van. And even though I was exhausted, part of me still yearned to go back out in the water and catch one more wave. We said goodbye to Kekoa and Noah, and planned to go out the next morning.

"I can't wait to get in the shower," Charlotte yelped as soon as we got home.

Kia was brutally sunburned but she cracked a smile anyway. "Surfing is just so peaceful," she said.

"Are you sure it wasn't Noah's voice that was peaceful?" Charlotte teased.

Kia tried to hold back a grin. "He's just a friend."

Charlotte rolled her eyes. "That's like me saying that Australian hottie was my brother."

After I took a shower, I put another bikini back on, and threw a cut-off shirt and some shorts over it. Kia had planned to do something with Noah. Charlotte had gone to help Tina out at her store, and Cyrus had passed out on the couch, so I decided I might as well go watch the contest.

As I examined the crowded beach, I realized the pier might be a better place to watch from. I found a bench on the pier and looked down at the scene below. A couple of tents were set up along the sand, and an announcer was sitting high up in a box seat, with a couple of judges on either side of him. At least five people were out there, all wearing bright rash guards. I felt someone brush against me and take a seat; I immediately drew back.

"I guess you had nothing better to do."

Maverick smirked as I shuddered.

"You have got to stop sneaking up on me."

"Why?" His eyes were playful. "Do I make you nervous?"

"No."

"That's a lie." He breathed, "I know I make you nervous. Just not like *that*."

"Don't flatter yourself. You don't have that effect on me."

I knew I was lying. I had crushed on a lot of boys, but I never felt shaky around them. But with Maverick, half the time I was afraid I wouldn't be able to get anything out of my mouth.

He just laughed, that same melodic sound, and turned his eyes to the ocean.

"That's Peter." He pointed to a boy out in the water wearing an orange rash guard. Peter was easy to identify. He had to be the smallest one out there, and his auburn hair wasn't exactly hard to miss, either.

"Can he surf?"

"He rips. But you should see me."

I made a face. "I have."

"Really?" he mused. "What'd you think?"

"You're pretty good..."

"*Pretty* good?" he bantered. "What does *pretty* good mean?"

"You know, it's like the nice way of saying kind of good."

"I don't know how to surf." Maverick smirked. "Would you teach me?"

I hadn't realized his arm was around me until I felt his tan hand brush against my leg. He measured my expression, just making sure I was okay. For once, I didn't feel suffocated by a guy. I knew he'd back off at any minute if I wanted him to, but I didn't, so I leaned into his shoulder and couldn't help a smile spreading across my face.

"Maybe," I whispered into his shirt.

I watched as Peter started to turn his board around; he was looking back at the sets of waves rolling in. I could tell these waves were going to be big; clear blue water was already starting to form. Peter started paddling.

"Would you go for that one?"

Maverick pointed at the wave behind Peter. It was the last one in the set, the biggest one. As it started to build, it seemed flawless. It looked as if it would never end. I imagined myself paddling for it and the feeling of the drop. If I had the opportunity, would I go?

"Yes."

I could smell the light scent of cologne on his neck mixed with the smell of the ocean, salt water, and sunscreen. I closed my eyes and lingered in it for a moment. He was tracing patterns on my leg, and I couldn't tell what they were. I realized his fingers looked a lot like an artist's: long and dainty. I remembered his board in the shop that he was cleaning the day I met him, all the abstract designs and bright colors.

"You paint, huh?" I guessed. My voice came out all breathy.

His hand became still. "How'd you know?"

"I'm good at reading people."

"I'd challenge that."

"Please," I bragged, "you're the easiest person to read."

He turned so he was facing me, his eyes fluttering to mine. "Alright then, read me."

It was hard to notice anything but those eyes. I felt like you could be miles and miles away from the ocean, but as long as you were with Maverick, you'd feel as if you were there. If the ocean was a person, it would be him: moody and confident and utterly flawless. And I could tell him he was hot, or that he was clever, or that he was a total jerk. But nothing I said could ever do him justice. There are some people you just can't put into words.

"I think you're the exact opposite of what you pretend to be."

He stayed still. I could see something flicker in his eyes but he masked it before I could tell what it was. He turned back to the ocean.

"Would you go for that one?" he asked, as a huge beautiful wave started to form in the water.

I wasn't paying attention to the question or the wave. I was too caught up in him: the softness of his voice; the way he watched the ocean so intently, as if it held secrets only he could know; his skin brushing against mine. The feeling was so overwhelming. I felt drunk off him.

"Yes," I murmured, but I wasn't looking at the ocean. And neither was he anymore. His eyes were locked on my lips and I wondered whether he had even heard what I had said. He looked lost in me.

I paused, measuring the moment. He didn't move any closer but he didn't move farther away, either. He just waited patiently, his eyes never leaving me. And I realized we were both drowning in each other, and it wasn't just about what waves you'd go on—it was about taking chances. That moment was so fragile and flawless, so I closed the space between us in one quick movement, like how a wave closes the space between the air and the rest of the ocean. I pressed my lips softly against his, and he crashed into me. We both pulled away with a smile playing on our lips, the sound of the ocean crashing in my ears. Most times you wish you're somewhere else, anywhere else than where you are.

But I melted into this moment; I let it pull me in like a wave.

SIXTEEN

The next morning, we spent most of the day out in the water again. As soon as I pushed through the soreness, I was fine. I didn't even notice how bad my arms hurt until after I had gotten out of the water. The whole time I was out there, I couldn't stop thinking about the feeling I felt when I kissed Maverick. I guess if I could compare it with anything, it'd have to be to riding a wave. Headfirst, diving, scary, exciting. New.

Kekoa had taken us out again, and this time he was also teaching a family of four from Sweden. They were not only extremely kind, but every time I turned around they were all on a wave.

You know what the ocean does to you, but you see it work in other people, and it's incredible. The effect it has. There is honestly nothing in the world quite like it.

"Hey, Charlotte and I are heading to Kae's to get a coffee. Do you wanna come?" Cyrus asked. It was late in the afternoon. I was so burnt from surfing, I was lying on the couch half conscious. I understood now why every time Cyrus came home from surfing, he was suddenly asleep.

"No, thanks. I think I'll take a nap."

Kia had gone to Noah's, Tina was working, and for once

the house was completely quiet. I drifted off as soon as the door clicked shut.

When I awoke, the house was still empty. I felt much more refreshed and even had a little energy in me. I knew Cyrus and Charlotte had probably gone on some adventure and Kia probably wouldn't be home until tonight. And who was I kidding? I was dying to see Maverick. But I had no way of getting a hold of him. Bored, I went upstairs and dug through my purse until I found the Nationals Surfing contest program. It was the contest at the end of the month everyone had been talking about.

I was flipping through it, still trying to figure out what I should do, when I landed on the page Maverick had signed. It was a picture of him doing an air. His messy signature was scrawled under it, and then beneath that, was a number. I gawked at it for a moment, and shook my head. Only Maverick.

I looked at the program, my phone, and then back at the program again. My hands felt shaky as I dialed the number and it started to ring.

"Hello."

"Maverick?"

He paused for a second. "Evie?"

"Come pick me up," I said playfully, trying to not let the nervousness sink into my voice.

"I'll see you in a minute."

My phone beeped a few times, letting me know the call

had ended. I was suddenly frantic. *A minute.* I quickly ran upstairs and looked in the mirror, trying to figure out how I'd look acceptable in a minute.

As I splashed the cold water over my face, I couldn't help but pause as I stared at myself. I looked so different. My eyes were brighter, my skin darker, my hair lighter. The dimples in my cheeks seemed to be more indented, as if they were now more noticeable from all the smiling I had been doing lately. A trickle of freckles ran its way over my nose. For the first time in a long time, I looked happy.

My bedhead was unmanageable, so I threw it up in a quick bun, brushed my teeth, and dabbed some vanilla lotion on my neck. When I glanced out the bathroom window, I saw a truck in the back alley. My heart jolted, and I swear it kept getting louder and louder with every step down the stairs. I opened the door to his truck and climbed in.

He smiled at me as I buckled my passenger seatbelt. "Hi there."

"Hi."

He reached a hand all the way over to me. "Why are you so far away?"

"I don't want to get cooties from you."

He pushed the center console up that was between us and patted the seat next to him. I unbuckled and scooted towards him. He looked tired, calm. He was wearing a hat flipped back, and it made his hair stick up in the front. I couldn't tell whether it was endearing or sexy.

"Where are we going?" he asked.

"I have no idea," I admitted. "Let's go on an adventure."

He smiled wider at me. "Adventure it is."

He put the truck into gear and started driving. His eyes were focused on the road again and I took advantage of the fact that he couldn't see me staring at him. His eyes always caught me first, but I found my eyes drifting to his lips now. I craved the feeling of them again.

"What were you doing when I called?"

"I had just gotten off work." He glanced over at me. "I was actually quite surprised that it was you."

"Why?"

"Well, first of all, you sound like a five-year-old on the phone."

I hit him in the arm. "I do not."

"Do, too," he teased. "And second, I had given you my number weeks ago. I was starting to think I had written the wrong one."

"Did it ever occur to you that maybe I just wasn't interested in you?"

He completely took his eyes off the road and moved his face closer to mine. I could smell the cologne lingering on his neck and the smell of the salty water in his hair. His lips barely brushed against mine, his blue eyes smoldering. "Regardless, you still called."

Every part of me felt dizzy. I was expecting to feel calmer around him eventually. I mean, I had seen him a lot. It was ridiculous he still made me feel so on edge. He made me act like a total fool.

His iPhone was plugged into the car. He scrolled through it and landed on a song. Foster the People sang back from the radio.

We were driving along the highway and the sun was just starting to turn to a sunset. Pinks and purples fluttered along the ocean water. It looked like a painting, too beautiful to be real. Maverick drove for a while longer until we wound our way into a cute little neighborhood.

"We're here," he said, stopping the car.

I looked around for a park or a coffee shop or something, but all there were was houses and a long, vacant street.

"Trade seats with me."

I looked at him, blinking.

"What?"

Before I could oblige, he was already picking me up and setting me down in the driver's seat. "I'm going to teach you how to drive."

"Funny joke."

The street was completely dark except for the lights coming from some of the houses' windows in the neighborhood. The glow from the dashboard illuminated his smile as he laughed at me.

"I'm serious. C'mon, it's easy."

I touched the steering wheel lightly. "But what if I crash?"

"You won't."

His confidence in me was cute. But I had never driven a car before. Although it didn't exactly seem like rocket science, it didn't seem like the easiest thing ever either. Plus, if I got caught, his, and my future license, would go out the window.

I weighed out the consequences. "How do you know?"

"I won't let you." His voice was like silk. "I promise."

I couldn't argue with a face like that. I settled into the seat, my feet barely reaching the pedals. It felt odd being the one in the driver's seat. As if I were a little girl graduating out of a highchair.

"Fine." I exhaled. "Teach me."

"Okay, press down on the gas."

I did what he told me to and the car lurched forward; my eyes grew wide and I braked.

He laughed. "Lightly. Just do it lightly. You're fine."

I tried it again, this time with less pressure, and the truck moved forward easily. I sped up a little.

"Good; now just start to slow down. There's a stop sign up ahead."

I braked as we approached it and the car jolted again.

"Sorry."

"Don't worry 'bout it. Just ease into the brake next time." His voice was patient.

I moved forward again and realized the road was a dead end up ahead. This time, I slowly started to brake, and the car stopped smoothly in front of a curb.

"Good job. Now drive over that curb."

I was expecting to hear sarcasm in his voice, but there was none. I looked over at him and his expression was completely serious.

"There is no way."

"Babe, you're driving a truck."

The word babe made me feel as if I was melting, and it was hard to stay stern. "I don't care if we were in a tank—I'm not driving over that curb."

"Why not?"

"Why would I?"

He sounded as if he were ten again. "Because it's fun."

"No."

He leaned over me with a smirk and moved his foot over so it was on mine, pressing on the gas.

"No!" I said, braking.

He was laughing now. "Babe, c'mon, just do it."

He pressed his foot down on mine again, making the car lurch forward; I hit the brake and yelled at him. He was just laughing at me, and suddenly I couldn't stop laughing either. He tried it again, and I realized he needed a distraction, so I pulled him closer to me and pressed my lips against his, gently at first. He took his foot off mine, and moved his hand away from the steering wheel, to the side of my face. Lightly brushing against my cheek, he pulled me closer to him. He tasted like spearmint and his lips were so gentle against mine, but there was still that craving. I was practically sitting in his lap but I needed him closer. I always needed him closer.

I sighed and forced myself to pull away from him. I felt as if I didn't belong in this world. With him. It was too perfect. That moment was too flawless to be able to hold in my hands, or wrap my mind around and that scared me. How could life be this good? This easy? It felt too good to be true.

I was waiting for something to go wrong. For this day to be a dream that I wake up from.

He watched me intently as I scooted back to my spot on the passenger side. I immediately felt the space between us, and it felt wrong.

"Why'd you leave me?"

"I'm right here." My tone was heavy.

He reached his long tan arm across and put his hand where the center console had been, his fingers reaching for mine. The radio was turned down but I could just make out the Beatles playing, I Want To Hold Your Hand.

Maverick started singing with the radio.

I couldn't help but laugh. "You should stick to surfing."

His voice was so light as he sang, and he was staring right at me, his fingers just brushing against mine. "I wanna hold your hand."

I pulled my hand away with a smirk and then I let it fall into his. I let my fingers intertwine with his.

Neither of us said a word, but we didn't need to. That feeling was so perfect. The feeling of simply not being alone. If this was a dream, then I'd spend the rest of my days trying to fall asleep to get back to it.

And I realized that moments were much like waves. They seem to go on forever while you're in them. Then all of a sudden, they're closing in on you. Then they're gone. And people are much like the ocean. Always changing.

So when given the chance, just stay still, just take it all in. Because if there's one thing that's true, it's that nothing ever stays the same.

SEVENTEEN

The sun leaked through the window every morning, the sound of the ocean coming with it. I found myself waking up with a smile on my face more often than not. As tempting as lying in my white linen sheets was, I knew that whatever was planned for me that day was way better than resting in bed. I couldn't wait to start the day. Showering and getting ready felt like a hassle. I threw on whatever clothes I spotted first, and makeup consisted of sunscreen, mascara, and lip balm.

Luckily, the getting ready part always waited until after surfing. The minute I woke up, I threw my hair up in a messy bun, tied my bikini as fast as I could and booked it downstairs, grabbing a piece of fruit for breakfast on my way to the car. Every morning consisted of a stop by Kae's to get a vanilla coffee, and then we drove straight to the beach parking lot.

Kekoa was always there before us. I was starting to think he never left. And he was never alone, either. He was always talking to a group of people when we pulled up; ninety-nine percent of the time they were foreigners. Some way or another, he'd convince them to go surfing. The amount of people we met in and out of the water was endless. Some spoke too little English to strike conversations with, or their accents were too thick to be able to understand, but it didn't really matter. We enjoyed each other's company. We shared something so much more than a conversation out in the water. We shared waves. We shared the ocean. And I was starting to believe that was a language that almost everyone understood. From the minute we hopped out of the van, we just wanted to get our wetsuits on and go.

I had discovered putting a wetsuit on was almost just as much work as surfing. I was getting faster at it, though. It still took Charlotte and Kia at least fifteen minutes.

The boys would always surprise us out in the water. We never knew whether they were coming until we got there. I'd paddle out and see Maverick on a wave, throwing airs like it was the easiest thing in the world.

Maverick and I had been sitting way out past the break when all of a sudden I saw a fin emerge from the water. Immediately, my mind went into overdrive. I had watched *Shark Week* too many times to count. I felt my heart start to beat insanely fast inside my chest.

Maverick did a double take at my worried expression.

"Babe, calm down."

The fin emerged again. My heart was now pounding in my ears like a drum.

"I can't."

He started laughing at me. "Are you serious?"

"Sorry I didn't grow up around sharks, unlike you." I glared.

He reached over to my board where my hand was resting and intertwined his fingers with mine. His tone was low, serious. "Just stay very still."

I swallowed hard and did as he said, trying my best not to make any movement at all. I looked straight at the nose of my board, not wanting to see what was going on in the water. I'm sure I had stopped breathing. I felt as if I might puke.

"It's gone," Maverick whispered, after what felt like an agonizingly long minute.

I let a breath out and looked back towards the water, only to see the fin was now even closer. Close enough to reach out and touch. I wanted to yell at Maverick, or hit him, but I was frozen.

Maverick started cracking up. He was laughing so hard, I swear it was bouncing off the water with an echo.

"Shut up," I hissed. "You're unbelievable. Do you want to get me killed?"

"Oh yeah, I can see it now. 'Dolphin Attack' written on the paper tomorrow morning."

As if the dolphins had been in on his joke, one jumped straight out of the water, clearly proving it wasn't a shark. I was angry with Maverick, of course, but I was too relieved it wasn't a shark, and too fascinated by the dolphins to scold him. There were at least five of them, and every minute they seemed as if they were getting closer and closer to us. Three of them kept leaping out of the water, doing flips and other tricks and then gracefully landing with a splash every time. The other two were more shy, and they stayed low, brimming against the ocean.

The pastel sky reflected the hues of pinks and purples in the water, as if the sky was merely dripping into the ocean. The smell of morning and salt water lingered in the air. The colors of the sky outlined the dolphins' fins every time they'd sneak up on us. One of the shy dolphins had gotten so close to me that I finally rested my hand in the water to see if I could touch her. She disappeared back under a wave, and a moment later she rubbed against my hand, and lifted her head just enough so I could see her dark, kind eyes.

People say magic isn't real, but I think they just don't see it. Magic is that moment between the sky and the sea. Magic is the second when we let the miracle that we are alive today really hit us.

Magic is the feeling of something wild brushing against your fingertips.

EIGHTEEN

Isn't it strange?

Isn't it strange how you can go from being absolute strangers with someone to then all of a sudden they are everywhere. All around you. Thoughts of them filling up your head. Suddenly, someone who you never even knew existed in this world, you can't imagine your life without. Falling in love with someone is odd. You don't fall in love with their looks. You truly fall when you start to study them. When you watch them from across the room, without them knowing. You watch as they play with their fingers, and run their hands through their hair, or bite their lip with nervousness. You watch them watching other people. When you see the way they get caught up in a joke that's told. You see them lose themselves in a story. Or the way their foreheads crinkle when something sad is said. When you study people, that's when you see all their sacred and secret parts of them. That's when you fall.

Watching Maverick was like watching a hurricane. I never was really prepared for his response to things. We didn't know everything about each other. I couldn't tell you his uncle's name, or his parents' names, for that matter. But in a way, we knew each other better than that. I had felt his eyes on me, too, when I was looking away. I wondered how often he had studied me without me knowing. And to be honest, most times it scared me. I had been raised by a family who taught me to not let anyone get too close. Then they'd see your weaknesses, your problems.

They'd see that your life wasn't perfect. That was my parents' worst fear after my brother's death. That other families would pity us. Or think less of us. Or watch us as we fell apart. I wondered whether my parents ever really experienced my brother's death. They spent so long burying it. Ignoring it. Pushing it away. They never let it hit them. It didn't seem fair that they could go around in a daze while I missed him terribly every day. I didn't have a choice. I missed my parents sometimes.

But most of the time, I didn't think about them much. I felt like when Clyde had died, part of them had, too.

~~

One night Kia, Charlotte, Cyrus, and I had all snuck down to the beach. Technically, no one was allowed on the beach after eleven p.m., and it was just pushing one a.m. Cyrus led us under the pier, crouching low at first. As we got closer to the water, he slowly stood up and did a double take. The beach was completely empty. No sound of beach quads or trucks. The only light was coming from the dimmed lights strung on the pier. I pressed my back against the sand, letting the wind toss my hair behind me.

The beach was a much different place at night. It was completely still. No sound of chattering teens, or volleyball players jumping and yelling. No beach towels spread out with endless bottles of suntan lotion and sunscreen. Only the ocean and us. The sound of the ocean caressed my ears, lulling me into a daze. I felt as if I was in a wonderful dream.

"Dance with me." I heard Charlotte's eccentric laughter and even though my eyes were closed, I could imagine she was pulling Cyrus towards her. Charlotte was humming a tune to an oldies song loudly, trying to suppress her laughter.

Then, I heard Noah's voice. I couldn't make out what he had said over Charlotte's loud humming, but I knew he was there, too. I opened my eyes and immediately searched for Maverick. I hated the sharp disappointment when I couldn't find him.

"Looking for me?" came a voice from behind me.

Like always, I was startled at first. I sat up in half a heartbeat. Maverick thought it was super funny to always scare me half to death.

"You're unbelievable." I pouted, even though secretly I was overjoyed he was next to me.

"I was just enjoying the view."

He took a seat beside me, and then laid all the way back, looking up at the stars.

I stared at him for a long moment.

"Are you going to join me down here or what?"

I rolled my eyes with a smirk, and rested my head back in the sand. One of the only good things about Moke Hill was the stars. When you found a clearing with no trees and smooth grass, you could lie there for hours at night, millions of stars glittering above you. Here there weren't as many. Just a few dotted across the sky, like freckles on a child. But they were still beautiful.

Sometimes, I feel like people are stars. Some flicker, some are dull, some burn powerfully, and some not at all. I imagined if Maverick was a star, he'd be the brightest one. He'd be so bright you just couldn't ignore him.

His blue eyes flickered to mine, so intense in the darkness it made my stomach feel all fluttery and uneasy. They burned their way over to me. And I knew I wasn't alone. Sometimes there are just no words. It's not even that you have something to say and it keeps getting stuck in your throat.

Sometimes there is just nothing to be said. Maybe we don't need to say everything; maybe we do in a way, silently.

That heat of another soul next to you.

That spark when your fingers find theirs.

That moment of hesitation right before you press your lips together.

This is the most important conversation.

A conversation that can't be talked about. One that can only be felt.

NINETEEN

From that day on, Maverick and I were basically inseparable. He'd often join Kia, Charlotte, and me out in the water every morning. During the day, we'd spend our time on the pier, watching other surfers, laughing with Kia, Noah, Cyrus, and Charlotte. I was constantly taking pictures. We'd lounge in Galligans, and help clean boards at Swells. Maverick would pull me in every time he was working and have me work with him. I'd help him look for boards and make calls.

Most of the time we just got in the car and drove. We never knew where we were going, but it didn't really matter. It wasn't so much about the destination than it was the drive.

There was almost never a day where we didn't get lost.

"You've lived here your whole life. Don't you know your way around yet?" I teased him, after we had been driving around for two hours trying to find the freeway.

"I *do* know my way around. I just like getting lost with you." He smiled playfully, biting his lip.

"You did *not* just get us lost for two hours on *purpose.*" I gasped.

"Oh, but I think I did."

My jaw dropped and all I could do was shake my head and look at him. The ice cream cone I had gotten earlier was starting to drip slowly down my hand.

"Hold on. You have something right there." I reached forward and with one quick movement, I smeared the ice cream from his ear all the way to his mouth.

"You did not just do that," he smoldered.

"Oh, but I think I did," I mocked.

He started laughing, the ice cream slowly dripping off his face and onto his shirt.

I leaned forward and started to kiss exactly where I had painted him. Just as I was about to pull away, I felt him slide the ice cream cone out of my hand.

"No!" I yelled, half laughing, trying to regain my grip on it. The ice cream was suddenly smeared all over my nose. His laugh was so contagious that I started laughing, until I was laughing so hard I threw my head back against the seat and I couldn't stop. The music was playing softly, and somehow it blended in so well with our laughter. The soundtrack of summer.

The spark every time he so much as brushed against me. My hair tangled and dipped in ice cream.

Young. In love. Free.

TWENTY

"I want you to meet my family."

Maverick and I had been out to lunch, sharing a bowl of Acai when he said it. And I immediately felt as if I had a strawberry lodged in my throat.

"Oh."

"Oh?" he countered. "Why do you look scared? I don't live with vampires."

"That's nice. I mean, that you want me to meet them."

"Today."

"Today?" I was hoping he didn't hear the utter confusion and nervousness in my voice. I had never met any guy's family before. Not even the little boyfriends I had in middle school. "But why?"

He was suddenly intent, closely watching my expression. "Because I want them to know you."

I started to play with my food, looking for any kind of distraction. "But what if they don't like me?"

"Evie." He reached forward and took my hand. He probably assumed it would calm me down, but really it just made my mind race ten times faster. "It's impossible not to love you."

I felt my heart jerk. "Stop lying."

He squeezed my hand and then pulled me up with him. "I'd never lie."

"That in itself is one."

"Okay, then," he said, his smile crooked. "I've never lied to *you*."

After resisting for a few minutes, I finally decided to just go with him. As we drove to his house, I had never felt so nervous before. Every knot in my stomach was twisted a thousand times. What if they thought I wasn't pretty enough for him? Or I said something stupid? Or even worse, I got there and couldn't get a single word out of my mouth? Maverick could tell how anxious I was. He held on to my sweaty hand as we drove, and didn't let go of it. After what seemed like a good ten minutes of driving, we pulled up to a pretty white house that was near the beach. It had a tall door and big windows, and a couple surfboards propped up against the matching garage. When I thought of where Maverick lived, I had always pictured a place like this. It was strange how much it fitted the image that had been inside my head.

"Ready?" Maverick asked me, as he turned the car off and pulled out the key.

"As ready as I'll ever be."

I had grown up with lawyers for parents, constantly going to fancy parties in big mansions with stuck-up people you practically had to bend over backwards to impress. And I could handle that. I could hold my own. I walked into those situations relaxed, even. Because I didn't care. But this was Maverick's family. Maverick was the boy I couldn't get off my mind before I went to sleep. The only boy who had ever given me the feeling of being in love. And if his family didn't like me, well, it'd be the end of the world.

He pressed his lips against my forehead for a long moment. "Don't worry."

Maverick didn't lead me to the front door, which I found kind of odd. He led me straight to the backyard, where a beautiful garden took up most of the yard. Large flowering trees and tall exotic plants wrapped around the white picket fence. I noticed a woman suddenly emerge; she squinted her eyes at Maverick and me and then started to make her way towards us. As she approached, I noticed she was blonde, tall, and thin. Just like Maverick.

"Hello there!" she said as soon as she reached us. Up close, she didn't look exactly like him. She had dark eyes, a heart-shaped face, and softer features. She was beautiful.

I went to hold out my hand to introduce myself, and I was suddenly embraced.

"We do hugs here, sweetie," she said smoothly, as she gave me one last squeeze and then released me. "Evelyn, it's a pleasure to meet you."

I was surprised she knew my name already. "You too..."

"Eleanor." She smiled; there was a smudge of dirt on her cheek. It made her look so much kinder than all those business grownups in suits I had constantly been introduced to.

"Your house is beautiful," I commented. I noticed that the backyard dropped down to sand and behind it you could just make out the line of the ocean. I was surprised by my sudden confidence. Maverick brushed his fingers against my hand and I could tell he had never doubted me.

"Thank you," she answered sincerely.

She turned to Maverick and pulled him into her arms. And even though she was on the taller side, he practically towered over her.

"How's my boy?" she asked, giving him a big kiss on the cheek. "I hardly ever see you anymore."

She caught my eye over his shoulder and said, "He's a fish," with a wink.

I laughed lightly, and Maverick made a face and hugged her back. "Speaking of fish, I was going to take Evie down to the beach."

"Okay, dear. Just be back for dinner."

As we made our way towards the trail that led to the beach, a little auburn-haired girl bounded up to us; she looked around nine. Her freckle-sprinkled face looked surprised at the sight of me. Her eyes were big and the color of chocolate.

"Hello," I said, kindly.

She blinked and her mouth pulled into a shy smile. "Hi."

"Noelle," Maverick said, ruffling her hair, "you don't have to be shy."

She put her lips up to Maverick's ear and whispered something.

"Yes, she's a girl," he replied. "And a friend."

She made a face as if she knew better than that and continued running to wherever she was off to.

"That's Noelle, my neighbor's kid. She's super shy."

"She's adorable."

"I adore her," he murmured, watching her disappear into the yard. "Almost as much as I adore you."

The trail led to a small slab of beach that perfectly met the ocean. I sat next to Maverick on the sand. It was still warm. The sky was just starting to shift colors, day fading into the evening. And as I watched it so patiently start to change, I realize not many people appreciate the middle. Everyone waits for the sun to rise or the sun to set. But what about the moments just before? Where everything is working to turn into something beautiful. Paints being spilled before a painting can be made.

I turned to Maverick and I could see the pastel colors of the sky in his eyes. It was as if the ocean was looking back at me: crystal blue and gray and green. It caught everything, including me.

His arm rested on the other side of me, and he ducked his head slowly down to my neck, letting his lips linger there for a moment. I closed my eyes and I couldn't tell whether it was the sun kissing my shoulders or him. I couldn't tell whether the wind was playing with my hair, or if that was him, too.

All I knew was everything around me was on fire. *I* was on fire. I couldn't tell where I ended and where he began. And everything else didn't really matter; it was all faded.

My fingers twisted into his hair and ran down his neck. They rested there as I pulled him closer. And finally, at the feel of his mouth, something in me seemed to calm. I let my other hand linger on his shirt, tracing the shape of his abs through it. We both pulled away breathlessly, and the world came flooding back. The sound of the waves, the seagulls chirping.

He closed his eyes for a moment, and then opened them, pressing his nose against mine. "You're going to drive me crazy, Evie."

"Am I?" I taunted him, sneaking in another kiss.

"You already are," he growled, kissing me back.

I laughed lightly and collapsed back onto the sand. "Gosh, what are you doing to me?"

His lips were softly brushing against my ear. "You tell me."

"You're making me all soft and...happy."

"Must be torture." The sound of his laugh tickled my neck, and I felt the light graze of his teeth against the side of my ear.

"Stop."

"Did I hurt you?"

"No, but you're making this impossible for me to be good."

His fingers were slowly tracing patterns along my legs again. "Be good."

He suddenly got up and started walking towards the water. The sun had just started to go down, the colors shifting into darkness. The moon was so bright, it made the water glitter.

Maverick pulled his shirt over his head in one quick movement, letting it fall to the sand.

He turned towards me, a smirk playing on his lips. "Are you just going to sit there and watch me get undressed or are you gonna come swim with me?"

"Swim?" I gawked at him. But I couldn't tell whether it was because of the sight of his bronzed abs, or the fact that he wanted to actually go swimming in the ocean at night. "There is no way."

He walked into the water without even flinching, and motioned his hand for me to come join him.

I shook my head.

"Baby, please." His eyes were suddenly so soft; his lips turned into a pout. Just the words sent my heart into overdrive.

"Tempting, but no."

He raised his arms over his head, clearly flexing. "Don't you wanna come swim with me?"

"Not really."

I rested my head back, trying to hide the smile wanting to break out behind my lips.

His eyes narrowed and he cocked his head to the side and looked at me; then all of a sudden, he was running straight at me.

"No!" I yelled as his hands found their way to my body and he threw me over his shoulder. "Maverick, put me down! Right now! Maverick, I'm serious!"

He laughed and started running towards the water.

"Maverick! If you don't put me down right now I'm gonna..." I tried to find something that sounded threatening. "I'm gonna..."

He stopped midway through the water and suddenly put me down. I screeched from the coldness of it.

"You're gonna what?" he asked, bringing his hands around my waist.

I tried to think of something to say, anything.

"I'm terrified." He laughed and then he fell straight back into the water, pulling me with him.

TWENTY-ONE

We showed up to dinner soaking wet. The long skirt and bandeau I had been wearing earlier was completely drenched. I felt mortified as I stepped onto the sleek wooden floors. The inside of the house was beautiful, too. All the colors of the walls were flowery and light: lavenders and beiges and soft browns.

I shivered as I sat at the dining room table.

"Should I even ask what happened to you two?" Eleanor asked as she set a large salad down on the table.

"Evie suggested we go for a swim. I tried to talk her out of it..."

Eleanor looked at me with disapproval. "Is this true?"

I felt flustered.

"No...no, I promise it wasn't my—"

Eleanor and Maverick exchanged glances and both started cracking up. I was already bright red, and I felt a flush of relief as I realized they were joking. That didn't stop me from giving Maverick a kick under the table.

"Cruz, did you go to Italy to get those noodles? C'mon, honey," Eleanor called.

A boy suddenly came through the kitchen door, carrying a big plate of spaghetti. He was even taller than Maverick, and he had very similar features, except he had a much darker complexion. He set the bowl down in the middle of the table and took the seat next to Maverick.

"Well, aren't you a pretty little thing." He smiled at me from across the table.

"Cruz," Eleanor said in disbelief.

Maverick practically growled, "Don't get any ideas."

I was sure I had turned another shade of red completely.

"I'm playin'. Chill." He reached out his hand. "Cruz. Nice to meet ya."

"Evie." I shook it quickly. "You, too."

He looked at least nineteen, and he had that same charming quality about him, that slight overconfidence that I had first noticed in Maverick. It was easy to see now where he got it from.

Eleanor put a heaping pile of spaghetti and salad on all of our plates.

"Waves were good today, huh, Mav?"

"If you like flat."

"Dude. I got so shacked today."

Maverick just laughed at him and rolled his eyes. "Yeah,

sure you got pitted, brah."

Eleanor turned her attention to me. "So Evie, what do your parents do?"

Maverick gave me a reassuring smile. I realized this was his first time hearing any of this. We hadn't talked much about my life back home.

"Lame question, Ma. You gotta ask the good ones, like have you ever done drugs."

"Cruz," Eleanor scolded him. "Sorry."

I took a moment to answer. "Both my parents are lawyers."

"Oh." Eleanor's voice was sincere. "That's wonderful. They must be busy."

Busy was an understatement. My parents were as career-oriented as they come.

"Yes," I agreed. "They're always gone."

"And any siblings?"

"One brother," I answered automatically.

It fell out of my mouth before I even had time to stop myself. And I felt the sting and the horror as soon as it had left.

"Well...I mean...I had a brother."

Eleanor's eyes shifted to unbearably sad as soon as she realized what I meant. "Oh...I'm so sorry to hear that, dear."

I could already feel the tears in my eyes, and the sudden feeling that it was harder to breathe. And then I felt Maverick's fingers intertwine with mine, under the table. For once, I didn't have to face that feeling alone. Just knowing he was there made it easier to pull myself back together. I was able to recover quickly, and even bounced back with confidence. I spent the rest of dinner asking Cruz and Eleanor questions and getting to know them. I was still freezing by the time dinner was over and Eleanor directed us to Maverick's room to change. Maverick pulled me through a hallway, to the last door on the left.

Maverick's room was exactly how I expected it. Painted light blue. A large window took up the back wall, where his bed was. A stack of CDs and a bar of surfboard wax was piled up on his nightstand. In the corner of his room was a desk, and a surfboard rack which held only a few boards.

A glimmer caught my eye, and suddenly I realized all the surfing trophies on the wall in front of me.

There were shelves and shelves of them.

"Wow," I breathed, as I took a step closer to read them. "Are these all yours?"

"Nah, my friends just keep them here."He said, sarcastically.

I felt him grab me from behind and his head rested on my shoulder, his laugh tickling my ear.

"You're amazing."

I felt him turn to stone behind me. "Did you just compliment me?"

I twisted in his arms so I was facing him. "I bet you get that a lot."

A smile was playing on the edge of his lips. "Maybe. But it actually means something coming from you."

The cold breeze leaked through his open window, making me shiver. He released me and walked over towards his dresser. After digging around for a minute, he pulled out a folded purple shirt with a sun design on it and a pair of soft pajama pants. "I hope this works."

"Wonderful," I said, taking them. "Now turn around so I can change."

"Yes, ma'am."

"No peeking."

"No promises."

I laughed and pulled the soft shirt over me; it barely skimmed the tops of my knees. I had to pull the pajama pants strings tight to get them to fit, and they were still a little loose but they worked.

"You can look now."

He turned around and just stared at me, his mouth slightly open. I realized he was wearing the same pajama pants that I was and no shirt. I looked myself over, thinking maybe I forgot to put something on.

"Why are you looking at me like that?"

He stepped closer to me, and I could feel the heat radiating off his body; his fingers were warm as he reached forward and moved the wet hair away from my face. "You're beautiful."

I felt as if there was an ocean in my chest, waves coming in huge sets, making my heart beat race. I didn't know what to say. I normally would have grabbed at his shirt and pushed him playfully, but my fingers brushed across his skin instead. He was too perfect. I still thought he might fade away under the tips of my fingers.

"Put a shirt on."

"Why?"

"I don't want your mom to walk in and think I'm trying to rape you."

"Don't worry," he murmured against my lips. "We're going somewhere else, anyways."

He went to his window and opened it all the way. "After you, my lady."

I gawked at him. "You want me to climb through it?"

"No, I want you to close it."

I rolled my eyes at him. The window was low; I hopped up and slipped through it easily and he was right behind me. We ended up in the yard again. He pulled me over towards the garage door.

"Oh great, this is where you kill me."

He nipped at my ear again with a laugh. "Precisely."

When he opened the garage door, I expected it to look normal. A few cars parked in there, a golfing bag maybe, or some bikes. But there was none of that. Instead, the whole space held racks of boards on the sides of the walls, and in the middle was a stand with a board lying on it. Right next to it was a counter with a bunch of tools.

"My dad was a shaper." He said to my confused expression.

I had never heard Maverick talk about his dad. I figured he was just really busy, like mine, and wasn't ever around much.

"What does he do now?"

"He died when I was eleven."

I could hear the pain in his words and my heart ached for him. Eleven took me back to the time I had drowned. To when Clyde had saved me. Who knew Maverick had drowned at eleven, too?

"I'm sorry."

It was a stupid thing to say because I hated when people said it to me. But I realized now it was the truth. I was sorry. I was sorry someone as good as him had to go through something as painful as that.

And it made sense to me now why people said it.

"Don't be."

"You're just like him."

He had the same features as his mom but I could tell there was something in him that was so different from her. Just in the way he was. It had to be his dad.

"Exactly. He loved the water. It's like he didn't belong here on land. When the cancer came, he drowned himself."

His fingers traced the rails of the surfboard on the stand. It was still messy, unfinished.

"Talk to me, Evie."

My heart felt heavy. "About?"

"Your brother."

His eyes were steady, patient. He reached across the board and squeezed my hand gently. I had never opened up to anyone about Clyde. It felt like a subject that was off limits. A place I'd never go.

"He was my best friend."

The words came out easily, as if I were talking about Kia or Charlotte. And Maverick just waited for me to go on.

"We'd always talk about leaving where we lived. And you know, some people are all talk but not him. He actually did what he said he would. He always kept his promises."

The words wouldn't stop now. They rushed out of my mouth like a flood of water. "He shouldn't have died. When you have a sibling, everyone says you'll have that person forever. That they're blood. That they'll always be there. But that's all bullshit. Because now he's gone and it's just me."

Thoughts were suddenly turning into words and they terrified me. I had never told anyone this. Not even myself. My heart was practically pouring out of my mouth but I couldn't stop.

"I drowned when I was eleven and he rescued me. But some nights I just lie in bed and wish he hadn't. Because now I'm here and he's not. He had this whole life here. It should've been me."

I felt the wet tears on my face before I even knew they were spilling out of my eyes, and I stood there in front of him. Completely shattered and ugly, and a lot like the board on the stand. Unfinished and messy. I expected him to be surprised or revolted or maybe both.

"I'm so happy you're here, Evie."

Then he reached out to me and for once I didn't pull away.

When people die, you're supposed to just forget about them. Like they were never really here.

Clyde was a lot like summer. No one appreciated him while he was here. But everyone missed him as soon as he was gone.

TWENTY-TWO

The next few weeks leading up to the Nationals contest, you could practically feel the anticipation in the air. As I lounged at Galligans with the gang, that's all they seemed to talk about. Who would show up, who would make it through the final heats, but most importantly, who would win. People from all over the world had come to Waverly for the summer, and that seemed to make the contest an even bigger deal. The wide variety of people poured through the surf shop all day, every day. Lanky girls with messy hair that spoke French. Couples from Russia. Burly boys from Canada. Young Chinese girls that barely spoke any English. I wasn't even sure half of them knew a thing about surfing, but they were all excited and eager to learn. They gazed at the surfboards as if they were made of gold.

Main Street lit up at night. The roads closed off and small bands came out, and everyone danced and sang, praising summer. We all knew she wouldn't be here too much longer.

Kia, Charlotte, and I spent the morning surfing with Kekoa and all of the boys. The rest of the day we lounged on the beach, soaking in every last drop of the sun until it disappeared behind the sunset.

Sometimes life can be so difficult. Like every minute is dragging, the days are so long. And every little thing seems to be a struggle. Like life is shoving you around. But then there are those days were everything is so soft, moments seem to melt together like honey, and everything is just so easy. As if life is just wrapping its arms around you and pulling you into its embrace.

Maverick was starting to get even more attention now that the contest was days away.
The first few days of the contest started, and it was very mellow. Maverick did well in his heats, always placing in the top spots. Everywhere we went, companies wanted to talk about sponsoring him, random people would come up and wish him luck, and the fan girls would constantly eye us and swoon over him.

As much as I wanted my alone time with him, it didn't bother me much. This was a huge part of his life and who he was, and I realized I'd have to accept it.

The last day of the competition, I woke up early and met Maverick at Swells to help him carry his new boards.

His sponsors had spoiled him. Five gorgeous boards were all sprawled out on the floor. He could have any one he wanted.

"Which one are you going to ride?" I asked him, picking up one that was colored like the American flag.

"None of them." He winked.

He unzipped a board bag that was dangling around his arm, and opened it up for me to see. Inside was a small black board. I looked at him, trying to figure out what point he was trying to make.

"It's the one that was in the shaping room. My dad started it and I finished it. Decked it all out so the sponsors don't try to kill me."

I let my fingers linger on the rails. "It's perfect."

"Isn't she?" He looked the board over and then kissed me on the cheek. "My two perfect girls."

I laughed and rolled my eyes. "Surfer boys."

As soon as we set foot onto the sand, a crowd of people were already moving in on Maverick. Guys with video cameras. Pretty girls. A lady from the local news.

We pushed our way through them without a word and finally arrived at Maverick's tent that was in the VIP area. Another crowd of people was waiting for him there. But these were all friends and family. They all exchanged handshakes and good lucks with him. Maverick thanked everyone and Cruz kicked everyone out so it was only his mom and me. Cruz took the role of coach.

"Your last heat is in an hour. You should go surf south side of the pier just to warm up a little. Get to know that board and then make your way over to the heat."

Maverick nodded; his wetsuit was pulled down to his waist and he was leaning over his black board, adding one more layer of wax to it.

"Who's the heat with?"

"Nathan Grover, that kid from Brazil, and Peter."

"Peter, your friend?" I asked.

"Yup," Cruz answered. "Friends play rough, babe."

Maverick finished pulling his wetsuit on. "Ready."

His mom gave him a hard kiss on the cheek and Cruz just patted him on the back. "Yew, brah. Let's go."

"Good luck," I whispered against Maverick's lips as he pulled me in for one last kiss.

"Thanks, babe." He smirked. "But I won't need it."

I found the gang all sitting on the beach, and I wedged myself through the crowd to go sit with them. Kia was cuddled up with Noah; Charlotte and Cyrus were both lounging on a towel, tanning. And Keegan and Vince were clearly checking out every single girl that walked by.

"How's he feeling?" Noah asked me as soon as I sat.

"Pretty confident."

"I'm betting on him," Keegan admitted.

Vince raised an eyebrow at him. "I'm betting on Peter. Those redheads are sneaky."

I could see Maverick, Peter, and two very tan guys all standing in bright rash guards right in front of us, their boards tucked under their arms. Suddenly a blow horn went off, and they all went running towards the water, jumping onto their boards and starting to paddle.

"In red we have Nathan Grover from Hawaii. In white, Francisco Ribeiro from Brazil. In orange, Peter Piccoli from San Clemente. And in blue, Maverick Greyson representing Waverly Beach."

As soon as the surfers got past the sets, they sat on their boards, keeping an eye out for any waves starting to form.

"It's pretty flat out there," Keegan noted.

"Looks like the surfer in orange, Peter Piccoli, found a small inside wave," the announcer's voice boomed.

Peter was suddenly up on a wave; it was small and weak but he did the best he could with it, doing a couple cut backs before it closed out on him.

As the time ticked, a couple of the other surfers had gotten a few small waves under their belt. Nothing too exciting but at least it was something. Maverick had caught two small waves, but after those two, he had just sat there on his board, waiting.

"What's he waiting for?"

The crowd was starting to grow restless, wondering what he was doing. He let a few waves pass him by, and he was still just sitting there, letting the other surfers take them as if it were free candy.

I thought back to the pier, how I had watched him find that perfect little diamond in the rough of a wave. And I suddenly understood his technique.

"We only have five more minutes of this heat left. Peter

Piccoli in orange is in first. Nathan Grover in red is in second. Francisco Ribeiro in white is third. And Maverick Greyson in blue is in fourth."

The surfers were much farther in than him, catching the waves on the inside. When a beautiful set started to form, far far out, they were all too close in to catch one of the waves. Their only choice was to duck dive under the sets and hope there would be another. But because Maverick was far out, he was in perfect position. He started to paddle, and then he was up, cutting back on a beautiful wave. He caught up with it just in time as it curled over him and he shot out, turning his board so he went over the top of it, landing on the water.

Everyone on the beach cheered, jumping up from the sand and shouting.

It was almost impossible to hear the announcer's voice. "Wow, and that was Maverick Greyson getting that beautiful barrel at the last minute."

The blow horn sounded off again, signaling that the heat was over and the surfers started to paddle back in.

Kia turned to me, her mouth hanging open. "He won!"

"Yew, he won, that's right!" Keegan shouted. He turned to Vince. "You owe me a beer."

"Hey now! I was close."

Noah hugged me. "Tell him I said congrats."

The surfers were making their way to the beach and

reporters and people were everywhere, running into the shallow water to meet him. Maverick had the biggest smile on his face, and just as I was about to reach him, another crowd of people pushed in front of me. I struggled to look past them, and when I did, I couldn't believe what I was seeing. Maverick was kissing another girl, his arm around her waist; her hands were thrown sloppily around his neck. I felt the physical pain in my chest before it even hit me. I let the crowd push in front of me. All the girls friend's were screaming in excitement, and I knew it had probably been a fan. I could hear Kia gasping, and then her hand was on my arm, and she was pulling me towards her, away from it, as if she was hoping I hadn't seen anything.

"Evie." Her voice was a million miles away. "Evie, let's go."

Maverick broke away from the girl finally and he was thrown onto two guys' shoulders, still smiling, on top of the world. And I was just standing there in the crowd, like any other girl, watching him in all his glory. His head was thrown back, and he was laughing. He looked like a chid. Like the same boy I had spent just hours before with. But this world he suddenly was in, was so much bigger than me. This was his story, not mine. So with an aching heart, I turned around, and kept on walking. Leaving the world where Maverick and I excised together, far behind me.

TWENTY-THREE

The next few days, my phone wouldn't stop ringing; every time I looked at it, Maverick's name and picture flashed across the screen. And every time it was getting harder to push Ignore. I didn't listen to his voicemails. I didn't want to hear his voice. I didn't want anything to do with him. What a fool I was to think he actually cared about me. A week passed and he finally stopped calling. And even though I had the beach, and surfing, and the surf shops to keep me company, there was a part of me that ached every time I walked downtown. I hoped I wouldn't see him; I prayed that I would.

It was ten at night when the doorbell rang. The weather had been so strange; a storm had been brewing, and the clouds had finally broken and it had started to rain. I was the only one downstairs. I didn't think before I opened it, and when I did, I instantly felt my heart drop.

"Hey you," Maverick said, as soon as I opened the door. His face looked relieved. "Is your phone broken or something?"

"No," I replied, pulling it out of my pocket and showing it to him. "Perfectly fine."

As always, he didn't miss a beat. "Oh, then you didn't get my calls."

The rain started to fall harder, and I wished I was outside, where the droplets could drown out my voice, my words. "I got your calls, Maverick. I just didn't answer."

His expression suddenly turned to confusion. "I don't get it...did I do something wrong?"

I wanted to hit him. I wanted to slap him as hard as I could across his flawless tan face. Then I wanted to kiss him so hard that this whole day would disappear around us.

"Just leave."

He stepped closer, reaching his hand out to me. "Baby, just tell me what I did."

"Don't call me that." I pulled away before his skin could touch mine. I knew if it did, I'd be screwed. I'd fall into his arms, the warmth of his touch, and all this strength I had managed to muster would crumble. He was close enough so that I could see that his eyes were darker today, heavy, too, from obviously another night of celebrating his win, and it made it a little easier to pretend.

"Is it about that stupid girl?" Maverick asked. "She basically attacked me as soon as I got out of the water. I don't even know her."

There was that ache again. Maybe he didn't and odds are he was right. But regardless, I was still leaving Waverly. What was I supposed to do? Our summer romance was ending. And damn, it hurt. I wanted to keep him forever. I wasn't done yet. If anything, this was just the beginning. But it was already time to let go.

"Look it's been fun and everything. But I have to be honest...I'm just over you."

I could almost hear Clyde's voice in my head. *"No one can lie like you; you make it sound like the truth."*

Maverick's tone was cold. "You're lying."

I practically choked. I had never been called out on it. Never had to keep going to make someone believe me. "Just because it's not what you want to hear doesn't mean it's not the truth."

He narrowed his eyes, studying me. "I know you better than that, Evie."

He reached for me again, softly, this time his fingers brushing against my skin. So close.

"Stop." My voice was getting louder as I pulled away again. "You don't know me at all."

I was good at pushing people away. But Maverick refused to stay away; he kept trying and trying.

He masked the hurt in his eyes with a playful smirk. "Let's go surf."

"I don't want anything to do with you," I snapped. "You were a challenge. It was fun. Now it's over. I'm leaving in a few days, anyway."

And there it was, that weak spot. With Maverick, I was

positive there was only one and I had hit it.

Because like me, he was so good at pretending. He just stared at me, lips parted, eyes turning murky like the ocean after a bad storm had hit. And the pain was so clear that I could've sworn I physically felt a knife wedging itself slowly into my chest. I wanted to grab hold of him, do anything to stop it, and although he looked extremely hurt, I was the one who had broken into pieces by my words.

"You're right. Just forget about it."

He turned and he was walking away and I could've stopped him.

His truck roared in the silence as he pulled out of the driveway, and I could've stopped him.

He was driving down the road, disappearing in the heavy rain.

And by then, it was too late.

They say you die twice. One is the actual death. And the other is when you look at someone for the last time, and you realize you'll never see that person again. At least, not in the same way.

TWENTY-FOUR

The ocean seemed restless as I paddled out. The waves were rough, and big, but we were leaving in just a few days and I knew I had to get as much surf time as I possibly could. So whatever the conditions, I'd be out there. A huge set broke right in front of me. I wasn't strong enough to keep my board steady, so the whitewash practically devoured me. I came up gasping for air, and tried to find my board. My leash tugged at my ankle but I couldn't see where my board had landed. Just as I caught sight of it, another set came rolling in, breaking right on my head. I was sent crashing down towards the bottom of the ocean again. I came up, clutching for air, exhausted from taking now two sets on the head. I saw my board but I was too tired to swim. I felt as if I couldn't breathe. It felt as if water was even in my brain.

"Evie," Kekoa yelled. "What are you doing? Get your board."

I ignored him and stood there; my head was pounding. I was tired. I didn't want to.

"Hustle, Evie."

I shook my head at him. I was tired of fighting for every little thing. When was I going to get a break?

The board was right next to Kekoa but he didn't grab it

and push it towards me. Instead, he glared at me and yelled something else that I couldn't hear.

I was getting ready to tell him to screw off when he finally grabbed my board and paddled over towards me. He tapped it once, hard. "Get up."

"I just wanna go in."

I could see another set was starting to build. If I took my leash off now, I could just swim into shore. If I got up now, I maybe had a slight chance of getting past it but if I waited any longer I would get worked in the set.

"Go ahead, give up. If you're gonna be a girl about it, at least go lie out on the beach in a bikini and look good."

"Excuse me?" I practically growled. I hopped up on the board just so I could prove him wrong.

"You're not going to make it over this set. You're gonna get worked."

I glared back at him and started paddling as fast as I could, pulling at the water so hard it felt like my arms were going to fall off. The waves were building in front of me, starting to crumble, and I just barely made it over the set. But I still made it over.

He was paddling right next to me, shaking his head, a smile playing on his lips.

"What's so funny?" I spat. I was pissed.

"She hasn't taught you yet."

"Who?"

"The ocean. You have much to learn, grom."

I tried to control my temper. "I don't understand."

"Evie." His voice was soft but strong. "I know you've been through things. Rough spots. But so have we all. Do you think the ocean cares about that? Do you think she cares if the boy you liked wasn't who you thought he was?"

"How do you know—"

"Does she?" he interrupted.

"I guess not."

"There's no guessing. She doesn't give a shit about any of that. Us surfers are treated equally out here. When we get a set on the head, when we get worked, do you see us sitting there and asking the ocean why me?"

I shook my head.

"That's right. You pull yourself together again, and you move on. Because the ocean isn't going to pause and wait until after you have your little pity fest to keep going. She doesn't stop for anyone. So you get your shit together, and you keep paddling, because you don't know what's up ahead."

I let his words sink into my head and I nodded. He was right. As blunt as his words were, they were true.

"Now with that being said, I see a beautiful wave that has your name all over it. So turn around, and start to paddle."

I did what he said, and again there was that feeling of my heart dropping as I felt the wave pick me up. As I pushed myself up and started to turn the board, it started gliding along the wave perfectly. And it was the same feeling as falling in love. You're breathless and it feels like the world stops for a second around you, and just as the wave starts to close, everything comes flooding back.

I realized that the ocean isn't just a playground. It isn't just a place. She's a teacher to everyone that comes. But only the ones who are truly ready to learn understand her lessons. She doesn't love, she doesn't hate, she doesn't pick favorites. She just pulls everyone in.

She is much like life. She is beautiful.

And in that moment I realized most importantly, she is home.

I knew I had to talk to Maverick before I left but I didn't know how. I couldn't press his number on my phone with shaky hands. I didn't have the courage to show up to his house. As hurt as I was by what he had done, I knew I couldn't leave things on the note I had left it.

Because Kekoa was right: like the ocean, life doesn't stop for anyone. And if I didn't find some kind of closure before I left, how could I go back to Moke Hill and put it behind me? Just the thought of going back made me sick. I couldn't believe it, and for the most part, I pretended I wasn't really leaving. I pretended it was just a sick joke going around.

I spent the last few days mostly in the water. And when I wasn't there, I was at Galligans, laughing with the boys, meeting foreign strangers, and having small talk with them. Or cleaning boards, helping sell clothes at Tina's store, or sneaking to the beach late at night.

But still, every time I closed my eyes, it was *his* that I saw. In those moments of him and me, I felt as if we could be forever. Infinite, even. But the ocean had taught me another thing: nothing, at least on earth, is forever.

TWENTY-FIVE

I woke up to the sound of the ocean like any other day. Except this day it was different; it was our last day. And so I lay in bed, closed my eyes, and let the sound of it caress my ears for a little while longer. We went downstairs to eat breakfast, like any other day, except this day was different, because it was our last day. And so I let the smell of pancakes fill my nostrils and I took in the sound of the coffee maker and Tina's happy voice as she greeted us good morning and asked us how we slept last night. I took in the sound of clattering plates and voices and noise. The sound of a new day.

We walked down to Main Street and I let myself feel drunk off the sound of music and people laughing. I breathed in the smell of surfboard wax and sunscreen and I didn't even mind the sweaty crowd of people on the beach with us. Because I knew I would even miss that. Cyrus took us into all the surfboard shops, and we announced that we were having a paddle out at sunset and then we'd be heading out. Kekoa had planned the paddle out. He said they had had one for Clyde after he had passed away but because I hadn't been here, they wanted to do another one. A paddle out is basically a surfer's version of a funeral. Except instead of mourning their death, it's a celebration of their life.

The sun started to set too soon. I buried my toes in the sand as I zipped up my wetsuit and grabbed my board. I couldn't believe the amount of people that were behind me when I turned around. Almost everyone from the surf shops had come; even Maddi had a purple longboard tucked under her arm.

Bright flowers dangled from everyone's hands as they walked across the sand.

Kekoa came over and hung a beautiful purple lei around my neck. "Ready?"

I took a deep breath. I think there are some things you'll never be ready for and this was one of them. But I nodded, because I knew I'd paddle back and I'd be alright.

I was the first one to make my way into the water. The ocean was so calm, it was as if she had known we'd be coming. We all were able to paddle far out into the middle of the ocean without any sets threatening us. We formed a circle, all linking hands. There had to at least be fifty people.

The pastel colors reflected in the sea. I let my hand rest in the water.

Kekoa said a small prayer and then splashed at the water and yelled, "Yew!"

And suddenly everyone was doing it, splashing the water towards the sky and then throwing their flowers in the middle of the circle. Kia, Charlotte, and I followed and we all smiled at one another. Was Clyde here with me now? Could he feel this?

The little boy from Galligans, Oliver, was sitting across from me. He had drifted towards the middle of the circle.

Everyone's attention was on him. He had the biggest smile on his face, and was clearly captivated by the scene. He threw his head back, and laughed at the sky. So young. So precious. I wished he could stay here in this moment forever.

I took my lei gently off around my neck and threw it in the middle of the circle, towards Oliver. I threw my head back towards the sky, too, with a smile, and let the last bit of sun kiss me.

This ritual wasn't about being sad; it was about celebrating a life. Everyone cheered and yelled. The sun was starting to go down, and Kekoa said a final prayer and we all started to paddle back.

As I was paddling, I couldn't stop smiling. I had never seen anything more beautiful. And then, I could feel him next to me, the heat of his body, letting me know I wasn't alone. I turned and it was Maverick; he was paddling right beside me.

"You came," I breathed.

"I wouldn't have missed it."

He reached over and touched my hand, and my heart started beating faster because of it.

And I realized I really did love Maverick. But love doesn't mean forever. It means for now, in this moment. And maybe that's okay, because maybe that's all we have.

I told Maverick to go ahead, and that we'd talk when I got to the beach. I sat on my board for a moment and I looked around at the people paddling next to me. You meet thousands of people in your lifetime, but no one really touches you. Then you meet a handful of people, and in the moment of meeting them, you can't even imagine what the future holds for you.

I'm not sure whether it's fate or coincidence but you can't let these people go.

No matter how much it hurts sometimes, you've got to let them stay in your heart.

Because these people become a part of who we are. They shape us, define us.

Summer was a haze, practically fading away. And I wished she could stay longer, but I knew I wouldn't appreciate her if she did. I closed my eyes and I thought about all the moments in the past couple of months. They had made me who I am.

When I opened my eyes, there was someone paddling towards me, built like a rugby player, blonde hair, freckles sprinkled across his skin. And then the sun hit his eyes.

"Clyde."

SEPTEMBER

Acknowledgements

If I were to thank every single person who has helped me in the process of writing this book, the list would go on endlessly. I'm sure you don't want to read a list that goes on endlessly. So I'll try to sum it up the best I can.

To my family, thank you for your love and unwavering support. It means the absolute world to me.

Thank you to my one of a kind teacher, Mrs. Tina. For continuously reminding me my story was one worth telling. You are still the only person I know that leaves me voicemails enticing me with ideas for my characters.

To my friends & sidekick, who not only have to hear me ramble about boys, but a novel, too.

To Rachel, thank you for constantly building me up in my faith, and giving me the gift of such a beautiful cover.

To my surf coach, Rich, for teaching me to always hustle, for introducing me to people from all over the world, and for always picking me up bright and early just so I could go catch some waves.

To my grandpa, because you believed. You will always be my number one fan. I hope there are book stores up in heaven.

To all the people and readers who inspired me along the way. You make this story real.

And last but certainly not least, to my main man, God. You are the greatest author there is. Because of You I am wonderfully and fearfully made. I am loved.
May all the glory go to You.

Mahalo.

I love you all times infinity

xxx

Greta

Greta Rose Evans

About the Author

Greta Rose Evans has one foot in the sand and the other in the Sierra Foothills. She is the middle child in a family of seven kids. Greta is a senior in high-school but finds it hard to focus on her studies when the waves are good.

To follow The Infinite Summer Series, or to connect with me online, visit:

www.facebook.com/GretaRoseEvansAuthor

Also, check out my friend Hannah Sanders' wonderful fashion blog.

www.razzberrykisses.blogspot.com

CPSIA information can be obtained at www.ICGtesting.com
Printed in the USA
BVOW05s1934010714

357923BV00003B/175/P